SOARING IN AIR

Magic of Nasci, Book #5

DM Fike

Avalon Labs LLC

ISBN: 9798561299261

Cover design by: Avalon Labs LLC

For Mary, who loves Ina and her world without knowing me.

CHAPTER 1

FOR THE FIRST time ever, I couldn't feel the storm.

Thunder booming above the roof kept me awake. I tried to sleep through it but failed. Blood pounded in my veins as the winds grew stronger. Even as a little kid, a sizzle deep in my bones alerted me to the storm's approach, long before I knew how strange that was. Yet now I cowered under a comforter, lightning casting my bedroom in white with each strike.

And I was completely disconnected from it.

The rain slamming against the window created an irritating hum, like rubbing an old wound. It made me want to itch all over. I couldn't take it anymore. Kicking back the covers, I marched to the living room's sliding back door. I had to press my forehead against the glass to view any details of the neatly trimmed lawn. Even then, the water poured down in sheets, obscuring everything beyond the fence.

A rational person doesn't hang around in an active thunderstorm, and for good reason. Taller objects won't necessarily save you since lightning might still choose you like a bad haircut. Even if you win that particular lottery, a concussive blast of shattered trees will kill you just as efficiently. About the best you can expect is to get completely drenched down to your underwear. Most people would have stayed inside.

I'm not most people.

I flung the sliding door open, the dull roar of pelting rain expanding into a rock concert of gushing showers. Barefoot and dressed only in a T-shirt and shorts, I squelched my way into the exact center of the yard. I brushed long strands of black hair away from my eyes, a losing strategy as rivers of water kept pushing them back into my vision. None of that mattered as I slid into a sigil stance: legs slightly bent, knees positioned slightly wider than shoulder width apart, and my hands poised at the ready to absorb and release the swirl of Nasci's energy.

And indeed, every flavor of pith presented itself in that moment. My toes sank into the mud underneath the grass. A howling wind whistled past my ears. Water coated my body like paint. I should have been able to grab all that pith and mold it into fire, the last basic element.

But no matter how hard I tried, my pithways wouldn't retain a single speck of magical energy.

I, Ina, former shepherd of Nasci, had really screwed things up. Believing myself infallible, I'd absorbed a bunch of bad pith from vile creatures that a psychopath named Rafe controlled. In doing so, I'd given him the power to hurt lots of people. I deserved all the consequences of my overblown hubris: my inaccessible magic, my mentor's abandonment, and even my self-imposed exile from the Talol Wilds shepherds.

But the lightning now seething above my childhood home tapped something primal within me. Before my epic fail, I'd been the only shepherd known to wield lightning. I felt broken without that familiar tingle of electricity, like I'd lost a limb. The storm taunted me with its memory, urging me to find it again. While my rational mind accepted that I could no longer control elemental magic, my heart would not let go.

So I reached up toward the exploding sky, willing lightning pith toward me. Maybe if a bolt struck me, my closed pithways would reopen. Maybe lightning would course through me again, and in its wake, the other elements would follow.

Maybe I could redeem myself.

"Gene!"

Rough hands shook me out of my trance. I was so bent on the storm that I hadn't even noticed my mother come outside. She hadn't bothered to put on a jacket, pulling me while wearing only a cream-colored nightgown, which clung to her like a second skin.

"Gene," my mom repeated, shortening my birth name of Imogene. "What on earth is wrong with you?"

Reality slapped me in the face. I wasn't a shepherd anymore. I couldn't just make things right with magic. Even if by some miracle I did absorb the lightning, I'd never managed to control it well. I could very well misfire and blow up the entire house with my mom and dad inside.

My hands fell back to my sides. "I-I…"

"For goodness sake." Mom threw her arm over my shoulder and ushered me back toward the house.

I endured her high-pitched rebukes as we dripped water all over the living room rug. She yelled variations of 'What were you thinking?' and 'You could have been killed" at me as I stood like a pale mannequin. Her ruckus brought my middle-aged Japanese dad out with towels, his face neutral as he helped dry us off.

"You're not a little kid anymore. It's time to grow up, Gene!" Mom thrust a manicured finger at me. "You can't waltz around the woods for the rest of your life."

She was more right than she knew. But no matter how long she lectured me, I couldn't take my eyes off the sliding glass door as the storm rolled away from the house. The lightning quieted into nothing, leaving only a thin drizzle of rain in its wake.

Like everything else, it left me behind.

CHAPTER 2

"HAGGARD!"

I whipped around to find a fierce woman with a blond ponytail and Amazonian build glaring at me. She stood in a pool of magma that snaked up her muscled legs, causing her fur-lined cloak to burst into fire at the edges. We stood on opposite ends of a long, rocky plain, the sky a swirling mix of sunset colors.

"Tabitha!" I yelled. "Get out of there!"

But as I rushed forward, I hit an invisible barrier. I couldn't reach her.

She scowled at me, the sharp lines of her face outlining her fury. "You did this to me!" The magma continued to claw up her torso, morphing her into an awful fiery version of herself, monstrous and golem-like. Soon, only her neck and face appeared human at all.

"No!" I cried, pounding on the wall I could not see. "Please, no!"

But I could do nothing as the magma ate her whole. Her human form collapsed inward like a sunken cake into the roiling lava below.

The sound of a cupboard door slamming jolted me awake. Gasping, I sat straight up in bed, my whole body shaking. I'd been having nightmares for a while now, but lately they'd morphed into the same horrible guilt-dream since I'd left the homestead. I gulped, reminding myself over and over again I hadn't killed Tabitha. That I wasn't to blame.

It didn't work.

The clock read seven in the morning. I was in Lynnwood, the Seattle suburb where my parents lived. Mom banged around the kitchen, a not-so-subtle human alarm clock. She'd mentioned last night that she would work the opening shift at the department store she managed and wouldn't be home until later in the afternoon. I pulled the covers back over my head. Given what happened last night with the storm, I had no idea if she planned on lecturing me again before leaving.

But she didn't. I heard her shuffle around for her purse and shoes, then the door to the garage banged shut. She clearly wanted to wake me up with the noise, but she had at least spared me a direct confrontation.

Her absence didn't alleviate all my discomfort, though. A long summer day stretched out in front of me, yet another meaningless rotation of the planet. With no plans and little motivation to make any, I trudged into the kitchen to forage.

The only good thing about coming home was the food. Shepherds consume mostly fruits and vegetables, adding carby breads and dairy only when the seasons allow. They're not vegetarians by choice but by necessity, since there's not a ton of wild game left to eat with shrinking animal populations. But here in the land of consumerism, I took advantage of a fully stocked kitchen to cook some eggs and bacon. I poured myself a large glass of orange juice as a chaser. The smell of breakfast wafting in the air, I placed my meal on the dining table alongside my mom's tablet so I could watch bad television as I ate.

I'd only gotten in one good bite when my dad came to evaluate the remnants of the coffee pot. Not finding enough brew to his liking, he filled it up with more water.

"Good morning, Imogene," he greeted quietly.

I swallowed before answering. "Morning."

Dad wore a button-up shirt and slacks, his faculty badge hanging on a lanyard around his neck. He must have been prepping for a late morning economics class.

Unlike my mom, my dad wasn't much of a talker, so I didn't expect much chatter when he sat down beside me, mug in one hand, briefcase in the other. I was still scrolling through the true crime documentaries when he surprised me by asking, "May we talk?"

I powered off the tablet. "Sure, Dad. What's up?"

He cleared his throat. "About last night…"

I knew where this was going. We used to roll our eyes when Mom would go overboard on some minor mishap, like me getting a 'C' on a history test. "You don't have to apologize for Mom. I know she means well."

He carefully placed his briefcase on the table between us, cracking it open a few centimeters. "I'm not apologizing for your mother. I'm worried about you."

I folded my arms across my chest. "I'm okay, Dad. Really."

He straightened in his dining chair, staring at a spot above my shoulder instead of my face. "You don't seem fine. You've spent more than a week moping around the house, watching TV and keeping to yourself. Add onto that your strange behavior last night, and we're both genuinely concerned about you."

I leaned back in my chair. "I told you when I came home, I had a falling out with my 'friends.'" The word sounded weird, even to me. With few exceptions, I hadn't really been friendly with most of my fellow shepherds.

Dad shifted from left to right a little, clearly uncomfortable, but he soldiered on. "Maybe you should seek professional help. I'm friends with staff at the Student Counseling Center on campus. I can schedule an appointment for you."

There wasn't a licensed practitioner in the entire state of Washington that could walk me through the emotional minefield of losing your magical abilities. "I don't need a shrink. I need time."

He sighed, rummaging around his briefcase. "Please keep it open as an option." He retrieved a set of papers, started extending them to me, but then hesitated.

Curiosity got the better of me. "What's that, Dad?"

His voice dropped to a whisper. "Your mom asked me to give you this. Take it as you will." He dropped the papers near his end of the table so I couldn't quite read the bold title on top.

His voice wavered as he stood from the table. "Remember, Imogene, we only want what's best for you."

Without further ado, he shuffled to the garage door.

I waited until I heard his car drive away before grabbing the papers he'd left behind. It was an application, not for a therapist, but for a job. A stocking position at Mom's store to be precise.

In the past, I would have gotten angry. Apparently, when life doesn't go my way, my dad thinks I should consult a shrink, and my mom's convinced a job will fix everything. But I didn't have the energy to feel anything but drained. I finished my food, not really tasting it, and settled down into a recliner. I chose to watch something happier than my own life, a 12-part documentary on a string of unsolved murders on the East coast, thousands of miles away from here.

* * *

Later that afternoon, my mom came home with groceries and found the application still on the dining room table. The only reason I knew was that, when I went to get a drink, I found it adhered above the fridge's water dispenser with a "Live Laugh Love" magnet, right where I couldn't miss it. Classic passive-aggressive Mom. I responded by barricading myself in my room.

Not that I felt proud of myself. At some point life would have to go on. Moping around my parents' house didn't solve anything. I just had no idea what to do next. I'd loved being a shepherd, protecting nature and slaying monsters, and I couldn't imagine a single thing in the modern world that would suit me as well. So I continued binging my show, not really paying attention to the details of the grisly murders.

The doorbell rang as Mom shuffled pots and pans around for dinner. "Gene!" she yelled. "Can you get that for me?"

I considered pretending I didn't hear her, but that would have been a true jerk move. Besides, maybe slamming the door in the face of a religious zealot would cheer my sour mood. I put down the tablet, emerged from my hidey-hole, and answered the door.

I did not expect Vincent Garcia.

Instead of his park ranger uniform, he wore an athletic shirt that hugged his chest, cargo shorts, and a baseball cap over his ebony hair. He took off sunglasses to reveal slight shadows under his dark eyes, lips set in a grim line. Behind him, he'd parked his personal silver Subaru on the street, a sign he wasn't here on official business.

"We need to talk," he said.

My mouth went completely dry. Although Vincent wasn't technically part of my shepherd life, we'd met through a series of unfortunate magical events. Despite my resolve to put the past behind me, a decent chunk of my heart soared at seeing him for the first time in weeks.

Still, he had no business barging in on my life unannounced. I swallowed to get some saliva flowing again and said, "I did like you asked. I called you after Mt. Hood."

He leaned toward me with a grimace. "You left a short message and then ditched your phone. I had no idea what really had happened. I've been searching everywhere for you."

I waved my arms at the house. "Well, here I am, alive and dandy at my parents' place." A question popped into my head. "Wait. How did you find me here?"

He at least had the humility to appear sheepish, although he grumbled, "I know your full real name. There's not that many Imogene Nakamoris running around."

My mom poked her head around the kitchen wall before I could reply. "Gene, who are you talking to?"

"Nobody," I said.

"A friend," Vincent said at the same time.

My mom homed in on Vincent's reply. She assessed him like a robot from the top of his head down to his shoes. Her face slowly morphed from one of polite distance to full-blown cheery customer service agent, teeth flashing as she scooted around the wall.

"Well, hello, there." She extended a hand to him. Vincent hesitated but eventually lifted his own arm to return the handshake. That's when my manipulative mother pulled him into a half-hug. "So nice to meet Ina's boyfriend!"

Vincent balked, seeking me out for some sort of an explanation.

"He's not my boyfriend, Mom," I said through my teeth. I knew exactly what she was up to. She'd tried to set me up before, believing that I lived on some sort of new age commune and ran around with a bunch of hippies. She must have been thrilled to have such a normal (and handsome) guy come knocking at the door looking for me.

My mom reluctantly let go of Vincent. "Don't just stand there, Gene. Introduce us."

"Vincent, this is my mom. Mom, this is Vincent. Now can you please—"

My mom cut me off, focusing solely on her new prey. "And what do you do for a living, Vincent?"

Wiping sweat off the back of his neck, Vincent replied, "I'm a police officer, ma'am."

My mom stiffened in horror. You could almost see the question marks forming in her brain about how I came to meet a cop.

"Game warden," I clarified. "He works with Fish and Wildlife. I'm not in any trouble."

"Of course not," Vincent said. Then he went too far. "In fact, Ina... I mean Imogene, has assisted me on a few cases."

"She has?" My mom's head bounced from me to Vincent and then back to me in confusion.

I hated that I had to choose the lesser of two evils here. My mom would freak out if she thought I'd gotten into any trouble with the law. Ultimately, I decided that was worse than the alternative.

Fighting off the urge to scream, I clenched my teeth and said, "We did kind of date for a while, Mom. Very casually. He discussed a few of his cases, and I made some small suggestions that helped him out. He's being way too modest." I paused to give him my best death glare. "Vincent could have solved them all by himself."

"Oh." My mom's pupils went back to their typical size. She grew a satisfied smile. "Then I was right. You guys were a couple."

Vincent's jaw dropped open. "Uh," he managed.

If Vincent felt completely adrift in the middle of this mad conversation, it served him right for showing up out of nowhere. I latched onto his arm before he dug us in any deeper. "We really need privacy, Mom." I stepped outside. "Sorry."

"Take your time!" she called sweetly, waving at us. I did not like the gleam in her eye as I shut the door behind us.

Standing on the front porch wouldn't be far enough away. Mom would eavesdrop on the wall. "C'mon." I marched him toward his car.

He coughed. "Why did you tell your mom we dated?"

"It's better than thinking I'd gotten arrested for tying myself to trees in front of bulldozers."

He stopped walking as realization dawned in his thick skull. "You mean, she doesn't know you're a shepherd?"

"Of course not! It's not something you can just tell everybody. You're not even supposed to know."

"But they're your family."

"Exactly." I stomped down the sidewalk, forcing Vincent to follow in my wake. "The less they know, the better."

"I guess I assumed you'd tell them."

"There's a lot of things you don't know about me," I said. "Like I didn't know about your ex-wife."

He went from confused to chagrined in an instant. "Okay, I deserved that one."

I rubbed my temples. "What are you doing here, besides giving my mom false hope that I might one day be normal?"

"But you're not normal." When he realized what he'd said, he threw up his hands. "In a good way! I mean that as a compliment. You're a nature wizard."

I didn't want to say it, but he'd backed me into a corner. I turned my head so I wouldn't have to look at him as I said, "Yeah, well, not anymore."

"What?"

He was going to make me repeat it. "I'm not a shepherd anymore."

He wouldn't let it go. "What does that mean?"

"It means like it sounds," I snapped. I noticed that my raised tone caused a flurry at the front window. Mom was spying on us. Straightening as stiff as a board, I said in my best quiet monotone. "The fight on Mt. Hood messed up my pithways. I can't wield magic anymore."

Vincent ran his fingers through his hair. "Oh, man. I'm so sorry, Ina."

His sympathetic reaction sparked a tear. I blinked it away. "Does everything make sense now to you, Vincent? Why I left Oregon? Why I ran back home? Are you satisfied now?"

He held out his pleading hands. "Maybe it's temporary. You might be able to heal yourself. Soak in a hot spring or—"

"No." I couldn't bear to tell him that even if I could get my powers back, the other shepherds would simply bind me after all the trouble I'd caused. Tabitha had died on Mt. Hood because of me. There was no going back.

"So, that's it?" Vincent asked. "You're giving up? Not even trying? Because there's something weird going on. Whatever happened on Mt. Hood didn't end with your phone call to me. It kicked off a flurry of seismic activity, not only on the mountain itself but across the state." He pulled his cell phone out of his pocket. "If you'll just take a look at some of this data—"

"No, Vincent!" I yelled. "It's over. I'm done with shepherd stuff. There's nothing I can do."

Then I hit his arm so hard, the phone fell down to the sidewalk. We both gasped. I hadn't meant to do that. I just wanted to get his optimism away from me.

Vincent stared at me for a long moment, jaw tightening. I broke off contact first, too afraid to face the judgement there.

He sighed. "I guess that's it, then."

I swallowed a lump, hoping he wouldn't see. "Yep."

He pocketed the phone. "I'm not sure what happened to you on Mt. Hood, Ina, but it must have been bad. Bad enough to change who you fundamentally are."

Why did everyone else think they knew what was best for me? "Maybe I finally realized what a screw-up I am."

But he shook his head. "You were never a screw-up. Stubborn, definitely. Infuriating, always. But the Ina I knew would do the right thing. She didn't run away from her problems."

"Sorry to disappoint you too," I threw back bitterly. "You're in good company on a long list."

He didn't answer that bit of self-pity, rounding the front of his car to open the driver's side door. "I promise not to bother you again. Hope that makes you happy."

Vincent drove away without so much as a backward glance. I stared down the road long after the Subaru disappeared from view, both thankful and heartbroken that he was gone.

CHAPTER 3

MY MOM COULD not stop grilling me about Vincent at dinner. Where'd I meet him? Why hadn't I ever told her about him? How did I meet such a 'nice' guy living on a commune? I gave her one-word responses, praying she'd get the hint. When she didn't, I excused myself from the table. Her snooping had somehow managed to ruin taco night, of all things.

Just because I'd escaped her questions, though, didn't mean I'd erased Vincent from my mind. What did he mean by 'seismic activity?' Did he know something I didn't? And what did that mean for shepherds? Too depressed to do anything, I reassured myself that it didn't matter. The past was done. My shepherd life was over. I had to move on.

My emotional state made sleep that night impossible, though. I tossed and turned for hours as the lazy sun set behind a bank of thick clouds. The house grew quiet as my parents settled down for the night. I heard the grandfather clock strike ten and then eleven o'clock down the hall, marking the agonizingly slow passage of time.

Frustrated, I finally crawled out of bed for a drink. I groped my way through the shadows, bumping into an ottoman and cursing. I found a glass drying in the rack next to the sink. When I pushed for water, the bright green light emanating from the dispenser made my eyeballs burn. I spilled water on the floor.

Irritated, I searched for a kitchen towel to mop it up. I cracked the refrigerator door open for light. I sopped up the mess and reached forward with the glass to refill the water when I came face-to-face with Mom's job application, glowing yellow thanks to the fridge bulb.

For one awful moment, I considered it. No one wants to work retail, but at least I'd make some money. Better than freeloading like a loser off my parents.

So, that's it? Vincent's voice demanded in my head. You're giving up?

I flinched away from the application as if it had bitten me. What was I doing?

Angry, and deep down frightened, I left my water glass on the counter. Still dressed in the same rumpled shirt and capris I'd worn during the day, I slipped on some sandals and grabbed a set of house keys. I left without a jacket and slipped out into the cool evening.

I had no specific destination in mind. That's the beauty of going for a walk. As far back as my middle school years, I took walks to relieve stress. There's something about breathing in fresh air and letting your feet guide you that calms a troubled spirit. I'd been cooped up in the house so long, I forgot how therapeutic it could be.

I also forgot how cold. Despite the fact that we'd reached the end of June, the nights dipped below 50 degrees. It wouldn't give you frostbite, but it wasn't fun for bare limbs either. I'd grown accustomed to not feeling cold by manipulating fire pith, but I couldn't do that anymore. The chill breeze caused sporadic shivers the farther I walked. I considered going back to the house, but it would take ten minutes and I'd made it to 196th Street. I figured I might as well keep going.

The normally busy streets lay dead this close to midnight. My mood improved as I trekked from one orange streetlamp to the next. However meaningless this journey, I was making progress. I came to the big intersection at Highway 99 and crossed to the gas station on the other side. The only other person in sight was a customer filling up a black pickup truck. Even with two lanes of traffic going in either direction, no cars zipped by.

That's when big fat raindrops pelted my head. I groaned as their frigid stabs created goosebumps wherever they struck. I should have grabbed a jacket. I spun around to go back home.

A sharp whistle cut through the air, an obvious catcall.

I jerked my head up. The bro at the pump returned the nozzle back to its place. He wore a jersey and sported a crew cut, the kind of guy you see playing pool with his buddies at a sports bar.

"Hey, girlie," he called again to me, opening his passenger side door. "Need a ride?"

I slapped on my best indifferent face. "Nah, I'm good. Thanks though."

He slammed the door shut, never taking his eyes off me. "But it's raining. A pretty thing like you could catch cold wearing such skimpy clothing."

Since when are pants and a T-shirt skimpy? "No really. I'm fine." I'd watched too many murder shows to ignore the alarm bells ringing in my skull. I couldn't take the direct way home because I'd come within yards of the bro. Instead, I twirled back in the opposite direction, putting some additional space between us.

I quickened my pace down the sidewalk, power-walking parallel to an empty office parking lot. I prayed the dude was just horny, looking for an easy score, but when I heard an engine rev behind me, I knew I was in deep trouble.

The black pickup truck soared out of the gas station, gunning for me.

Adrenaline pumping, I took off in a sprint, zooming past the glassy windows of a bicycle shop, my mirror twin running in step beside me. As I cleared the last pane of glass, the truck's front fender entered the reflection. I veered to the right down a side street, hoping to change direction faster than the vehicle could react. I headed straight toward a dollar store.

No such luck. Tires squealing, the black pickup made the turn. As he sailed into the same parking lot, he wouldn't even have to jump the curb to clip me.

In that split second, the only cover I could find was a short metal fence on the far side of the lot that separated the store from a wooded area. A truck couldn't drive through trees. Praying I wouldn't slip in the ever-increasing rain, I raced for those tree trunks.

With the pickup gaining on me, my foot tapped onto the lowest bar of the fence, stepping upward toward the second rung like a ladder. Then, in one fluid motion that would have made an Olympic athlete proud, I launched myself up and over the top railing into the forest beyond.

I expected to land on the other side and keep running. Instead, I discovered the fence had been built because the parking lot bordered the edge of a steep, weed-filled slope. My limbs flung wildly as I fell an extra fifteen feet. If I hadn't spent years training on mountainsides, I probably would have broken a bone or two. As it was, I landed so hard into a bush that I saw stars.

But at least the truck didn't come barreling after me. It hit the metal fence with a screeching crash but did not break through. A car door slammed, and the bro swore profusely above me. Headlights trickled down into the foliage, illuminating leaves around me. I wasn't about to stick around for him to spot me. Scrambling on all fours, I dove deeper into the woods.

Branches ripped at me, stinging my sides. Fortunately, I only had to run fifty feet through bramble before I found a paved path. Intending to avoid more scratches, I followed it into an obviously well-maintained park, the kind that preserved a slice of wilderness within suburbia. It took my muddled brain several minutes to comprehend where I was—Scriber Lake, not far from the main road.

A white and blue flash suddenly overtook the sky, silhouetting the trees. A loud crack issued soon afterward. Rain truly poured now, like a faucet spun open.

"Wonderful," I mumbled. Another thunderstorm. I had no phone to call the police, no way to get home safely. It was just me, the woods, and the storm against a lunatic. Stumbling down the pavement, I had to find a way out of this situation as quickly as possible.

The path led me to the park's namesake. Scriber Lake wasn't impressive at all, more wetland pond than majestic body of water, a quiet place for the people of Lynnwood to walk their dogs during the day. In the middle of the night under dark rolling clouds, it became the perfect horror movie scene, the kind where the music decreases to single low notes. I found myself smack dab in the middle of a dark rainy night with low lighting and a murderer hot in pursuit.

I wouldn't be a victim. I dashed forward to find

more cover under the trees.

A flickering light across the water caught my attention. Thinking it a flashlight, I ducked down low, peering toward it. Unlike a normal light, it twinkled on and off, too ethereal for something powered by batteries. Its brilliance intensified as I stared at it, a beacon beckoning me across the lake. I had no idea what it could be until another flash of lightning lit up the entire lake.

The bolt revealed a quadrupedal mammal, larger than a mountain lion but with enormous triangular ears. She sported a red coat with silver breast, pupils gleaming as they stared at me. Two paintbrush-like tails swished behind her, sealing her identify.

"The fox dryant," I breathed, standing up to my full height. After everything I'd been through, she chose now to reappear. I didn't understand why, but it didn't matter. A buzz hummed at the edge of my fingertips. She cocked her head at me, mouth slanted in a grin. I wanted to reach out and touch her, but she was all the way across the water.

Then I felt it. The lightning storm raging above me. My first pith sensation since Mt. Hood.

I didn't have time to celebrate that fact as rough hands yanked me from behind. I screamed as one set of fingers tightened around my waist, the other across my throat. I struggled, unable to see the pickup bro, even though I could hear his raspy threat.

"You're going to pay for the truck, bitch."

A sizzle sparked somewhere deep in my gut. I didn't hesitate. I pulled on it, forcing it up and out through my fingertips. I'm not even sure if I wrote a sigil as I released it toward my attacker in a shattering boom of light and fury.

"Charge this!" I bellowed.

Then the world went dark as I collapsed under the weight of my own magical explosion.

CHAPTER 4

"MISS?"

I groaned as someone shook me. The light receded, giving way to formless shadows that eventually morphed into vague blobby trees. Finally, a concerned mustached face assembled in the haze above me, the shaking sensation intensifying.

"Miss, wake up."

Leftover adrenaline from the assault shot through my veins. I screamed, and the mustache immediately backed off. I lurched in the opposite direction.

"Get away from me!" I cried.

An older gentleman with rough skin held out his hands in a gesture of innocence. He wore a one-piece maintenance uniform and carried empty trash bags. Keys looped around his belt buckle. Behind him, birds sang their morning tunes under a partly cloudy sky, bits of blue poking through.

"Now hold on a second," he said. "I work here."

It took me a second to realize he wasn't the bro from the black pickup, even though I stood by the little wetland marsh. "I'm still at Scriber?" I asked, more to myself.

The maintenance man answered nevertheless. "Yep. I just opened the gate. And Miss, you have to leave. It's illegal to camp overnight in the park."

Out of habit, I opened my pithways to absorb bits of earth pith. To my surprise, it worked. The heavy weight of earth, though slow, seeped into my core, connecting with the dirt underneath my bare calves.

"Whoa!" I examined my hands as if I'd never seen them before.

The maintenance man sighed. "I'm too old for this."

I ignored him, searching for a breeze. I reached out to absorb it, and air pith crept into my system, making me feel lighter and settling in over the earth pith.

"Booyah!" I cried. I scrambled to stand, muck and dirt sluffing off me.

The maintenance man took a step forward. "I really don't have time for tweakers this morning. If you'd wake your friend and get out of here, I won't call the cops."

Friend? I glanced beyond the maintenance man to discover a crumpled form laying in the dirt behind him. Gasping, I realized it was the bro from last night.

Just the thought of the attempted assault sent waves of nausea crashing through me. I wanted that creep as far away from me as possible. I acted on that impulse, channeling all my newly acquired earth pith into my palms. Drawing a square sigil with a slash, I snapped my wrist, releasing that energy into the ground below the bro. Dirt clogs detonated upwards, and the impact sent my assailant sailing in a perfect parabola. His limp body landed hard twenty feet away on a fallen log. Never regaining consciousness, he slid over the bumpy wood into Lake Scriber itself.

A strangled cry escaped the maintenance man's mustache.

Smiling in satisfaction, I announced, "He's not my friend."

Then I took off down the path back toward the road.

My gratification lasted until I found myself strolling past the bro's wrecked truck, still in the dollar store parking lot. Someone had placed a towing notice on it. I shivered in the chill as the morning commute crowded the street. No one gave me a second glance, too fixated on their upcoming jobs and school. But I suppose that's life. Everyone's concerned about their own stuff.

As I walked back to my parents' house, I tested my reopened pithways. I absorbed pith wherever I could: a little puddle of water here, rubbing against some bare dirt there, and a steady breeze all around. That gave me the three elements I needed to create fire pith. Drawing a triangle with a cross overlay transformed all that natural energy into a slow heat, making my T-shirt and capris perfectly comfortable attire.

Reopened pithways or not, I was not operating at full capacity. The flow remained restricted, storing less pith than I was used to. After leaving 196th Street for more residential neighborhoods, I risked an experiment. I tried lighting my entire hand on fire, then moving a large decorative boulder on someone's lawn. Nada. I didn't have the juice to execute either.

Still, I was grateful for any abilities at all. I supposed I should thank the mysterious fox dryant. We shared a strange history, dating back to my first experience with ken, the sight that allows me to observe magic. She appeared before me in the woods on a camping trip. That sighting prompted me to search for more mystical creatures in the forests surrounding my college town, and it's through those trips I eventually met Guntram. She didn't resurface again until well into my shepherd training, when she caught me practicing lightning in the desert by myself. She helped me properly wield lightning for the first time, and although I have trouble controlling it, that last encounter paved the way for me to safely, though slowly, improve my electrical gift.

To further complicate matters, no one besides me had ever seen the fox dryant. Guntram insisted that since she wasn't a documented dryant, she could not be real. The other shepherds thought me crazy for even believing in her. While I knew her appearance at Scriber Lake meant something important, no one else would care.

I arrived back home to find the garage empty, both of my parents already gone to work. They apparently hadn't noticed my absence because they hadn't bothered leaving me a note. The smell of coffee lingered as I poured myself a glass of water. I stared at the job application attached to the fridge, the catalyst for last night's walk.

I'd been right. No retail job for me, not with my magic returning.

But then what? I couldn't just rejoin the Talol Wilds shepherds either. They'd want me bound for my previous transgressions. I wasn't about to go waltzing back to the homestead only to have Guntram seal my pithways for good.

That left only one option: Vincent.

I powered up Dad's computer, nestled on a built-in shelf in the dining room. Vincent had mentioned something about Mt. Hood and seismic activity. I wished now that I'd let him give his spiel, but at least I could do a little Internet sleuthing. Typing on the browser's search bar, I entered "Mt. Hood" and clicked on news.

I did not expect a deluge of recent news articles.

My jaw dropped as I scrolled all the headlines on the first page. "Mt. Hood Rocked by Earthquakes." "Sudden Uptick in Tremors Scares Locals." "Oregon State Officials Reassure Public after Seismic Flurry."

I tried to reconcile it all. Everything that had gone wrong in the past few months had climaxed on Mt. Hood. The shepherds had been guarding a dome of lava, the blood of Nasci herself. Rafe, a bound shepherd with a murderous edge, had tricked me into helping him access it. He made me believe I was helping my fellow shepherds by amassing a bunch of vaettur pith, while in reality, it only fueled his own power. He used that awful pith I'd cleansed to attack the shepherds and reach the lava dome. If not for an augur named Tabitha, he might have absorbed it all, killed the shepherds protecting it, then gone on a murder spree across Oregon. Tabitha threw herself in the lava to stop him, though, cutting short both of their lives.

That should have ended all the drama on Mt. Hood. The lava dome had vanished. There was nothing left on that mountain but horrible memories.

I clicked to the second page of news links and flinched at the top headline. It read, "Earthquakes Collapse Site of Wonderland Resort," dated several days after Rafe's demise.

My palms went dry. Rafe had hated Wonderland because of the environmental damage the company's new resort would cause the mountain. Filled with dread, I clicked for the whole article.

An in-depth read confirmed the worst. There had indeed been an earthquake after our fight on Mt. Hood, triggering a landslide that buried most of the original construction site. I gasped at a photograph of a backhoe stuck twenty feet in crumbling earth, a dead insect with metal legs sticking up in the air.

"It makes no sense," CEO of Wonderland Resorts Lee Foster quoted for the reporter. "Our geologists conducted extensive studies in the area. The area should have withstood the earthquake's relatively moderate magnitude."

When pressed whether construction of the resort would go on, Foster insisted he planned on seeing the project through to the end. He refused to comment on the ongoing protests against the resort.

I leaned back in the creaky office chair. Earthquakes rarely occurred around a lava dome because shepherds guarded it, but Rafe's attacks could have caused something we could not predict. Were the quakes a natural consequence of our battle? Or worse, did Tabitha's sacrifice into the lava have something to do with it?

I had no immediate answers, but I wasn't at a complete dead end. Vincent had mentioned other seismic activity across Oregon. The Internet didn't have much info on that, but then again, Vincent had access to governmental databases I couldn't view online. I had no idea where Vincent went after our little chat, but with my pithways open, I could travel through wisp channels again. They connected locations all around the Pacific Northwest. I could catch up with him in Florence, Oregon and take it from there.

I rummaged through my bedroom for my standard shepherd gear, a hoodie and shorts. I felt naked without a charm necklace, which I normally wore for extra pith and defense, but I hadn't thought to bring one with me when I left the homestead. At least I found a pair of double A batteries in the junk drawer, just in case I needed to whip out some lightning. I wrapped them in a plastic bag along with a newly issued credit card and shoved them into my kangaroo pouch. Lacing my hiking boots by the door, I twisted the front doorknob to leave.

I realized belatedly that I couldn't run off without letting my parents know. I ambled back to the kitchen, unsure of how to tell them. I tried writing a note on printer paper, but I threw three attempts away in rapid succession. Regardless of how pushy or judgmental my parents were, they cared about me. I couldn't wait around until they came home, but I could at least call one of them.

My father is notoriously bad about answering his phone so, cringing, I picked up the house line (who still has these?) and called my mom's cell. She answered on the second ring.

"Gene!" she exclaimed. "Why are you calling me at work? Is something wrong?"

I took a deep breath, mentally prepping myself for the inevitable. "Mom, I'm leaving again for Oregon. You might not see me for a while."

I rubbed my temples against the litany of outrage that followed. "What do you mean 'leaving?' You just got back! What about getting a job? You better not be going back to those hippie friends of yours."

I began to regret my noble decision. "I'll be fine, Mom, I promise."

"Fine? Do you think you were 'fine' when you showed up on our doorstep a few weeks ago, morose and depressed? You've been holed up watching TV since you came home. I swear, Gene, whatever they did to you won't get any better. Once someone shows their true colors, they never…"

This would never end. My fingers twitched to hang up, but then an idea popped in my head. It was either a great idea or the worst idea, but it was the only card I had left to play.

Biting my lip, I interrupted, "I'm actually going with Vincent, Mom."

Her monologue immediately halted. Five whole seconds passed without a peep from her, then ten. I listened for the sound of a loud thud, indicating she had fainted.

"Mom?" I asked.

"Well." She cleared her throat. "I guess… well. Okay. Okay, then, Gene. Maybe… maybe you should go then."

I raised an eyebrow. "Really?"

"I mean…" I could hear the hesitation in her voice. "I mean maybe." I imagined her in business casual attire, an angel on one shoulder, a demon on the other. One argued that Vincent seemed like a nice guy who might take care of me in the long run. The other hated me out of her sight and rallied for me to stay. I had no idea which position represented the angel and which the demon.

I decided to play to her warring conscience. "Vincent's a police officer, Mom. He asked for my advice again. It's like a job."

I'd said the magic word. "A job?" she repeated. But then her voice lowered suspiciously. "But I thought you said you didn't help out much with those other cases."

Oops. I had said that. "I couldn't emasculate him in front of you. Cops have their pride and all."

"Oh." She took the bait. "Yes, I suppose that's true. A job."

Time to reel her in. "But I gotta go now, Mom. Sorry I can't wait until you guys get home. You'll tell dad for me?"

"Sure, honey, I will. And Gene, know we'll always be here for you, even if you've got no one else."

She always said those lines when I left home. They usually irritated me. Who wants to admit defeat and live with their folks? But after everything I'd been through the last few months, those words really gave me the warm fuzzies.

"Thanks, Mom." Then, awkwardly because I'm bad at open affection like my dad, I added, "Love you."

"And I love you, honey." Unlike my words, her declaration came out naturally. I guess I never give my mom enough credit for that. She may be a nag and a bit pushy, but she loves without condition. She hated my lifestyle and still looked out for me. I really was lucky to be born into that.

CHAPTER 5

SIMPLE WORDS CANNOT express the pure joy that coursed through me as I cut across the wilderness. Sure, my pithways hadn't fully opened, which dulled my senses like listening to a conversation underwater, but the ability to absorb and release pith gave me a contact high. I conjured light breezes and drank water directly out of the air simply because I could. I waved at a passing parade of mama skunk and her kits. I swore I could feel Nasci's heartbeat pounding beneath me in the earth. I didn't realize how much I missed that part of me until it returned.

I took a long route back, adding hours to my trip. It allowed me to savor the experience, true, but it also minimized chance encounters with other shepherds. Guntram and the others wanted me bound, so I took only the most remote wisp channels, their soft blue twinkling lights teleporting me vaguely southward. My path even took me near the Bitai Wilds border, a neighboring desert region not monitored by the Talol shepherds. But whether sagebrush and sand, or sun and seaside, my pithways sang.

I arrived at the outskirts of Florence by late afternoon, a decent walk away from Vincent's apartment. Shepherds don't have a lot of mobility in cities, where concrete and power lines cut off a lot of natural pith. It's one of many reasons why most shepherds avoid civilization. Me, though, I love me some modern living. I enjoyed the flat walk along the backstreets, the sidewalks mostly to myself as everyone else used cars.

I couldn't quiet my burgeoning excitement at seeing Vincent again. If you'd asked me straight up about him, I'd probably babble about how we met under less than ideal circumstances (he shot his firearm at me, I almost left him for dead in the forest, you know, the usual). In reality, though, our chance relationship had blossomed into something far more complicated. He obviously liked me on some level. No man who tracked me down after all the shenanigans I'd pulled could feel nothing for me. And I definitely cared about him, despite my attempts at burying it. The groggy kiss we'd shared before I left for Mt. Hood made me blush just thinking about it.

But what were we exactly? I'm not sure I could label it. He was a game warden who lived in the "real world." He did not dabble in magic. I am (or was?) a shepherd with feared lightning capabilities who definitely should not mingle with the magic-less throng. Between that and our largely incompatible lifestyles, it left a lot to be desired, romantically speaking.

I cut through one last quiet neighborhood and through a swatch of trees before I emerged into Vincent's apartment parking lot. He lived in a modest two-story complex with external door access only. The new building was utilitarian, the kind you only lived in for a year or two at most, unless you were a bachelor too lazy to move.

When I didn't spot Vincent's silver car, I groaned. Maybe he'd stayed in the Seattle area on vacation or something. Despite not having a clue when he'd get back, I had nothing better to do. I nestled in some nearby foliage to spy on his unit for the remaining daylight hours.

I didn't have to wait for long. Vincent came rolling in from the busy roadway only twenty minutes later. My heartrate quickened as he parked. I stood to greet him when out popped not only Vincent but a second person from the Subaru's passenger side. A brunette in a low-cut tank top and booty shorts giggled at something he said. Her gorgeous locks fell in perfect waves to mid-shoulder, a light summer breeze completing that runway model vibe. She grabbed a petite designer piece of luggage from his trunk.

I'd caught a glimpse of her only once before, and that time had not been pleasant. Vincent's ex-wife.

My pulse pounded now for all the wrong reasons. Vincent's relationship with his ex had been a huge point of contention between us. Right when we were getting serious, I discovered them having dinner together completely by accident. Vincent swore up, down, and sideways that they were just friends, but the way she batted her eyelashes at him, you could tell she didn't share that opinion.

And with Vincent's easy smile back at her, he sure didn't look like he minded the attention.

Heat rising up my neck, I couldn't decide who I wanted to strangle first. So, he came to visit me yesterday in Seattle, but it took him all of one day to hook up with his ex? If Vincent was truly over his ex-wife, as he desperately claimed, he wouldn't have rebounded to her so fast. Blood boiling, I swirled on my heels to leave without being seen.

If she hadn't let out a dismayed gasp, I might not have eavesdropped on the rest of their conversation. "But I thought I'd come upstairs with you."

Vincent frowned. "We've been over this, Christy. I'm not interested in you that way anymore."

She glared at him, scrutinizing his face even as he turned away. "You've been acting strange the entire drive back. Mopey. Distracted." A scowl spread on her lips. "It's a girl, isn't it?"

He set his jaw but said nothing.

She took a few steps forward. "Did she reject you or something, Vinny?"

I stifled the urge to gag. Vinny? Ugh.

His grimace indicated he wasn't too pleased with the name either. "It's none of your business."

"Sounds like she dumped you. Who cares?" She

hooked a hand through his arm. "That means you're available. C'mon, Vinny. I'm free. You're free. It's not like we haven't done it before. Let's have a little fun, just for tonight. No strings attached, I promise."

For an eternity, the world stilled around me. I couldn't feel a smidge of humidity, not the slightest breeze. Everything hung motionless as I waited for Vincent to answer.

He did not even hesitate. He pushed Christy off him. "You know I'm not that kind of guy."

Christy's tone shifted from seductive to angry. "Am I not good enough for you unless you're madly in love me with?"

Vincent sighed as she stalked away from him toward a green sedan parked nearby. "Christy," he began.

"You can keep your stupid knight-in-shining-armor routine!" she yelled back at him. "Life's not video games and comic books, Vincent. There's no such thing as true love. One day, you're going to have accept that or be lonely forever."

He made two fists at his side. "So what, Christy? Should I have let you cheat on me forever? Just shrug my shoulders and say, 'Oh well, that's life?'"

She flung her car door open and tossed the luggage inside. "I made one mistake! I was young, dumb, and insecure. And now you won't ever let me live it down."

Vincent unclenched all his muscles in surrender. "Christy, we don't have to keep dragging up the past. We were awful together. We're better off this way, as friends."

"Keep telling yourself that, Vinny, but one day you'll regret it. And then it'll be too late." She shoved herself into the car. The engine roared to life, as angry as her mood. She rolled down the window to get in one last word as she drove off. "Enjoy your holier-than-thou life."

Her tires squealed as she sped out of the parking lot.

Vincent walked away from the argument with only a slight hunch in his shoulders. He unlocked his apartment and disappeared inside in anticlimactic fashion.

It took me a lot longer to recover. My emotions went to war with one another. On the one hand, what caused Vincent to drive around with his ex the day after he visited me in Seattle? But on the other, dear lord, he'd really laid the smackdown on that scheming chick. In the end, the latter sentiment won the battle in my brain.

Vincent hadn't been lying to me. He wasn't dating his ex.

Honestly, Vincent could have slept with her, and it wouldn't have meant a thing. I had told Vincent in Lynnwood to go fly. He didn't realize I would show up on his doorstep to reverse that decision the next day. Most guys I'd ever known would have jumped at the chance for unattached sex.

With a lightness in my step that had nothing to

do with air pith, I jogged up the stairs to Vincent's apartment. I gave a brisk knock, then tapped my toes waiting for him to answer.

He'd only been inside minutes but took his sweet time answering. I considered rapping again when the door finally inched open. He didn't have a peephole to identify me, so he charged ahead with, "Look, Christy, I meant what I said. I—" Then he noticed me instead of his ex, and he nearly tripped over the weathering strip. "Ina?"

"Hi!" I waved, grinning from ear to ear.

Vincent glanced around wide-eyed. "I'm sorry, I thought you were…" he trailed off as he realized what he might let slip.

"Your ex-wife?" I finished helpfully.

He smacked his hand against his face, groaning. "I swear, it's not what it looks like."

I stopped him with an upturned palm. "You're right. It's not."

He glanced at me through splayed fingers. "What?"

I leaned toward him. "I watched your whole argument with her in the parking lot."

He went back a half-step. "You did?"

I nodded. "You're not sleeping with her."

He took it as a question and not a statement. "Of course not! I may be an idiot sometimes, but I learn from my mistakes. I gave her a ride to Seattle so she could visit some friends, but nothing else happened. My goal was to find you, I swear."

I placed a hand on his wrist, interrupting his tirade. "I believe you."

He let his hands fall back to his sides, his defenses shriveling. "Oh."

For a long moment, we stared at each other, two awkward people having no idea what to do next. I wanted to say so much, but for once, couldn't find any words.

He finally broke the silence. "How did you get here, Ina?"

"Wisp channels. It took me all day."

His eyebrows came together. "You said you didn't have magic."

I raised a hand and drew a sideways S. A breeze hit my back and blew straight into Vincent's face, tossing his ebony hair off to one side.

"Turns out I was wrong. But more important than that, you were right. I can't give up. Not now."

My rumbling stomach butted into the conversation. I grinned sheepishly, patting it. "And I guess I'm hungry too."

Vincent's face melted into a soft smile. "I can't let you starve on my doorstep." He grabbed keys from inside and locked the apartment. "Let me buy you dinner."

I didn't argue as he led me to his car. The interior still held the chill of air conditioning, a stark contrast to both the heat outside and the warmth inside my blood. I had no idea what would happen between us, but I trusted Vincent explicitly as he steered his car toward downtown Florence.

CHAPTER 6

VINCENT ASKED WHERE I wanted to eat, so I mentioned my favorite downtown seafood joint. Located on the riverfront, the clam chowder there tasted like heaven on earth, and I always tried to stop by when I could.

Unfortunately, everyone else within a five-mile radius had made the same plan. Tourist season had arrived on the Oregon Coast. We parked in a large public area and waded through window shoppers, slow moving families, and dogs on leashes just to reach the restaurant. By then, dinner rush was in full swing. The line to enter the restaurant extended out across the little harbor bridge and almost to the street. We wouldn't get a chance to eat there for at least an hour, and my poor empty stomach couldn't wait that long.

Vincent noticed my hangry mood and ushered us farther down Bay Street, searching for an alternative. He led me to a squat yellow building with a glass brick doorway and a sign boasting several varieties of beer. Vincent said he knew someone on shift who would get us a table quick. Reminding myself that most beach pubs can't screw up fish and chips, we ducked inside.

The signs weren't kidding about the beer. Bottles of them covered not only the wall but the ceiling too, hanging down like frat house stalactites. The rest of the décor centered around drinking said bottles, with wooden signage for local brews and artwork featuring—you guessed it—more beer-related paraphernalia. Throw in a couple of pool tables, slot machines (because why not) and a flat screen TV flashing a soccer game, and you had a typical Oregon sports bar.

A hostess greeted Vincent as an old high school classmate, his insider. She scored us a private corner booth not far from one of the TVs. After the hubbub of ordering was complete, Vincent slouched, swishing a glass of water in his hand.

His dark eyes pierced mine. "Tell me everything. From the moment you left for Mt. Hood."

Vincent knew I'd gone off to warn the shepherds of Rafe, but he had no idea what happened on the mountain. I exhaled slowly. "It's a long, ugly story."

"We've got nothing but time."

I laid it out for him. Normally I would have fudged some details, but given everything Vincent had done for me, he deserved the truth. I told him about the four elemental golems Rafe had created using the pith I'd inadvertently cleansed for him. I mentioned the injured shepherds, including the Oracle, the leader of the Talol Wilds. I took a deep breath before plunging into how Tabitha had given her life to seal the lava dome shut, preventing Rafe from absorbing unimaginable magic power. I did not mince details as I outlined being buried alive, even when Vincent clutched his glass so tightly I worried it might break. I finished with Darby, Tabitha's eyas, saving me, and the shepherds' decision to bind me for my role in Rafe's rampage. Since I'd already done so much damage by absorbing golems, I'd lost access to my pithways anyway, so I ran away before they could finish the job.

After I got to the point where I'd made it back to my parents' house in one piece, Vincent asked, "So, you believed your nature wizard days were over?"

I nodded. "Until last night. I went for a midnight walk in the rain. Ran into an awful dude-bro in a pickup. He ended up chasing me a few blocks trying to kidnap me."

A vein pulsated on Vincent's forehead. "You're shortening my lifespan here. Why would you go walking alone in a city so late?"

I threw up my hands. "I needed to think, okay? My entire life was ruined. I thought I'd have to work retail until I keeled over dead from boredom. I didn't mean to go looking for trouble."

"Yet, it always seems to find you."

"And I always kick it to the curb. I jumped a fence into a public park and the dude-bro wrecked his truck trying to catch me. The storm worsened in the park." I paused for dramatic effect. "Lightning flashed. And who should appear but my good friend, the fox dryant. I electrocuted that guy straight into unconsciousness." I chose to leave out the part that I'd knocked myself out too. No point giving Vincent a heart attack.

Vincent perked up at this. "The same fox dryant the other shepherds don't believe exists?"

"One and the same. And now my pithways are open again. I'm not back at full capacity, not even close, but it's way better than zero."

Vincent considered my story with furrowed eyebrows. "What does all that even mean? Why would the fox dryant do that for you?"

"I don't know, but it's gotta be a sign. The fox dryant has only ever appeared to me twice before —once to give me ken and a second time to save Guntram against the cockatrice. She must believe I'm worthy of being a shepherd."

"I don't doubt you," Vincent said slowly. "But it's going to be difficult if your peers want to bind you."

"Which is why I came to see you. I saw the news about an earthquake leveling the Wonderland construction site on Mt. Hood. You mentioned it's not the only place experiencing strange seismic events."

"Yeah." Vincent pulled his cell phone out of his pocket. "The USGS has reported a lot of activity throughout the Cascades." He showed me a digital map of the range, several large red dots noting different medium magnitude quakes.

I bit my lip. "I mean, there's a fault line there. Maybe they're normal quakes?"

"Our seismologists don't think so. They've flagged these incidents as highly unusual with no discernible pattern. It's got them so stumped, the Forest Service has been put on alert in case it's indicative of a larger disaster."

The waitress brought us our food then, interrupting our conversation. We passed condiments, napkins, and utensils. I settled into my fish and chips while Vincent chowed down on a burger. I gracefully added a ketchup stain to my hoodie, thankful that black fabric tends to forgive most stains.

As we dove into the meal, Vincent spouted off earthquake statistics from his phone. I admit that my mind wandered, focusing on the flickering images of the TV instead. Someone had changed the station to a local news broadcast, 3D boxes and fonts zipping across the screen to announce the day's top stories. I took a sip of pop.

The word 'Wonderland' flashed across the screen in huge white text. "Jim Borden, CFO of Wonderland Resorts, was found dead this afternoon," the anchorwoman announced.

I choked. Carbonated beverage went up my nose.

"Ina?" Vincent patted my hand as I sputtered. "Are you okay?"

I waved toward the TV. "Look," I managed around a cough.

We both focused our attention on the screen, the headline "Resort Executive Drowned" scrolling by.

Vincent gasped. "The hell?"

A photo of Borden and his wife taken at some ritzy gala event dominated the screen. They pulled off the "aging power couple" look well, impeccably dressed in tuxedo for him and simple black dress for her. He had a neatly trimmed beard with no hair on top, sporting a cocky smile as he raised a champagne glass to the camera.

"Jim Borden had been visiting the Oregon Coast with his wife Sharon. The two took a walk on Heceta Beach around ten o'clock this morning. Although Sharon insisted they stayed a safe distance from the shoreline, she claims a wave bore down on them out of nowhere, dragging her husband into the ocean."

"Did you know about this?" I whispered to Vincent.

He shook his head. "No. I've been off duty the last few days."

The graphic switched to a whimsical logo of a stylized skier swishing down the flowing lines of a W in the shape of a mountain. "Wonderland Resorts has experienced major financial setbacks this month after an earthquake destroyed their latest project, a new outdoor recreation area on Mt. Hood. Environmental groups have labeled the new resort a travesty given its location on previously protected forestland."

The screen shifted to a reporter in a windbreaker standing beside a beach. Police cars had parked directly on the sand not far behind him. "It was here on Nye Beach where Borden's body finally washed ashore. Local officials say it is a stark reminder never to turn your back on the ocean." The interview continued with the reporter talking to a police officer, who went through a bunch of tips on how to keep yourself safe while on the beach.

As the broadcast moved onto a story about glass floats in Lincoln City, my mind went into overdrive. "Can you believe that?"

Vincent shrugged. "It happens. You know better than me how unpredictable nature can be. And if there really is a nature goddess living beneath our feet, maybe it's her way of dishing out karma."

I shook my head. "Nasci doesn't work that way. She's not vengeful."

Vincent shifted uncomfortably. "Then how about a mere mortal? Your shepherd friends might want to settle a score for their lost comrade."

"Absolutely not," I snapped. "To do so would break shepherd code."

"Then I guess that leaves coincidence. Some other sort of justice meting itself out in the vast universe."

I wasn't so sure, but I let it go. Vincent outlined the handful of earthquake hot spots that had cropped up around Oregon, stretching from here to the middle of the state. I wished I could say I concentrated on his data, but my mind wandered to Borden and his untimely demise.

I didn't like coincidences.

CHAPTER 7

THE SUN HAD fallen into the ocean as we finished our meal, signaling the end of a long day. The crowd on the riverfront had thinned, but the remaining bustle forced us to thread through a throng back to Vincent's car. Passing couples holding hands and soft rock blaring out of random kitschy storefronts made me conjure up all those lousy love songs about oft-remembered summer flings.

"Where are you spending the night?" Vincent asked as he clicked to unlock his car.

I waited until we'd both buckled up inside. "I dunno. I hadn't planned that far ahead. I could spend the night in the woods. My fire pith should keep me warm."

Vincent started up the engine. "You sure that's a good idea?"

"I've spent the night outdoors by myself plenty of times." I bit my lip. "Although it's possible a dryant could find me and alert shepherds. If they found me, they'd bind me for sure."

Vincent's eyes locked with mine. "You're welcome to stay with me."

My heart skipped a beat. "You mean, at your place?"

"I have a futon in the living room you can use," he said in a neutral tone, glancing behind the vehicle for pedestrian traffic. "It's a logical solution."

If I hadn't noticed his face redden, I might have assumed Mr. Smooth didn't have any emotional investment with me crashing his pad. Despite all our talk of shepherds and strange geological phenomenon, we'd avoided any real discussion about the state of our relationship.

I dreaded my next words but had to say something. "Doesn't that make things complicated?"

The setting sun hit his face as we rolled onto Highway 101. Vincent pulled down the driver's side sun visor. "I vote we keep things strictly platonic."

Platonic. A part of me relaxed in relief, but the rest bristled in annoyance. I didn't appreciate either extreme, so I settled on a tense, "Oh?"

Vincent stiffened. "I think we've got enough going on without adding another layer of problems to the mix, don't you? It keeps things simple."

"Sure," I replied in a monotone. "Simple."

Vincent risked breaking his gaze from traffic to glare at me. "What exactly do you want here, Ina?"

I balked, not expecting the direct approach, but I'd been honest with him so far. Why stop now? "I'm not sure," I admitted without the attitude. "I'm just confused."

Vincent's glower melted into sympathy as he focused on the road. "Then you understand where I'm coming from. I have strong feelings for you, but given everything that's happened, I'm not sure if I should pursue them or not."

A cold shiver spiked through my arms. I rubbed them, blaming the air conditioning. I'd spent so long wondering if I should let Vincent into my life, but it'd never dawned on me that he could have similar doubts about me. Who could blame him? I'd put him through the wringer since I'd met him —from bludgeoning him with a whale corpse to my latest rejection of him in Seattle. He had every right to have second thoughts.

"Okay, that makes sense." I tried my best to sound positive and not in the least crushed. "Let's focus on one thing at a time."

He must have accepted this as the best response because we said nothing more as we pulled into his apartment complex.

Once we walked back upstairs, Vincent held the door open for me. His apartment looked exactly like I'd last seen it, a threadbare pad with no adornments on the off-white walls. He flicked on a standing lamp to cast an orangish hue throughout the living room. On an adjacent wall, his flatscreen TV and game console gleamed a dull black. Some dirty clothes were lumped together in a pile to one side, but otherwise everything appeared clean. He shuffled the laundry into the hallway as I removed my muddy boots near the door.

"You need a shower?" he asked from around the corner.

I glanced down at my slightly wrinkled clothes. Since I could regulate my temperature again, I didn't sweat as much, and my body felt mostly clean. "No thanks."

He returned with sheets wrapped in his arms. "I hope you don't mind if I jump in. It's been a long day of driving. Then I better go to bed because I have an early shift tomorrow." He gestured toward the futon. "You know how to fold that thing out?"

I patted its rough cushions. "Yeah, a college buddy had one. It's no big deal."

He handed me a blanket with a flat pillow folded on top. "You can use this as bedding. Feel free to watch cable as long as you want. The remote's on the stand, and you can snack on anything in the kitchen."

"Okay."

We paused for a few awkward seconds. Vincent eventually broke it by excusing himself. He locked himself in the bathroom, the sound of running water filling up the hallway.

Normally, I would have gladly taken the op-portunity to watch TV well past midnight, but I'd nursed that bad habit too long at my parents' house. A day of traveling and sigil drawing had drained me. I pulled out the futon and settled the blanket around myself, wondering if I should at least wait to use the bathroom before I fell asleep. But I never got a chance, drifting off well before

Vincent finished his shower.

* * *

I stood at the edge of a boiling pit of lava, searching frantically for Tabitha. I knew she had fallen in, although I had not witnessed it. I touched the red-hot surface, retreating when it burned my fingertips. She had to be in there somewhere, sealing the dome shut. Maybe I could still reach her.

"Tabitha!" I yelled. With one agonizing thrust, I shoved my arm into the viscous fluid up to my elbow, instantly losing all sensation in my arm. "Tabitha!"

I've always thought you were weak-willed and not worthy of being a shepherd. Her final words rang in my ears.

Prove me wrong, haggard.

A blinding light struck my face, the bubbling noise of the lava drowning out all my other senses. I fumbled around without context, trying desperately to orient myself.

I crashed onto Vincent's hard carpet in a tangle of blue blanket.

Blinking, it took me a second to realize the light that blinded me hadn't been a dream. An LED lamp in Vincent's bedroom flashed through the doorframe and struck my eyeballs like a focused laser beam. The bubbling noise came into focus too, the sound of a coffee pot gurgling as it heated up water. The only sensation I couldn't completely account for was the continued numbness in my arm.

Probably slept on it wrong, I thought as I crawled back up onto the futon.

Vincent appeared in the hallway, bedhead spiking in all directions. He guided a toothbrush up and down his teeth, a line of toothpaste poking out from the corner of his mouth.

"Ima?" He mispronounced my name through the brushing. "You okay?"

I waved him away. "Just not a morning person."

Vincent raised an eyebrow but shuffled away to spit in the bathroom sink. I waited until he emerged a few minutes later with combed hair before using the bathroom myself.

I returned to the living room. Vincent poured himself a mug of coffee. "You want some?"

I nodded, gladly accepting his additional offerings of milk and sugar. I cupped it in my hands, letting the steam float up through my nostrils as Vincent tucked his gun and wallet away. It was only then I noticed he wore a full black police uniform, not the beige park ranger one I'd seen him don before.

"What's up with your cop costume?"

He glared at me. "It's not a costume. I have different uniforms for different purposes. Today I'm out on patrol. And I gotta go now if I'm going to make it on time."

I glanced at the microwave clock. "5:40 in the freaking morning?"

"Shift starts in twenty. I might not come home until right before dinner. You good for the day?"

I shrugged. "I'll figure something out."

He drummed his fingers on the countertop. "You don't happen to still have a cell phone, do you?"

"Nope." The p-sound of the word popped out, making my reply sound more flippant than I intended.

Vincent frowned. "Then I suppose I should pick you up a new one before I come home. I don't like not having a line of communication to you."

"I've been okay languishing at my parents' house. I'm sure I can languish just as well here."

Vincent opened his front door. "If nothing comes up, I should be home around four. Can you be here then? And please, Ina—" he paused at the threshold, "—don't do anything dangerous."

* * *

Don't do anything dangerous. Yeah, sure.

The nerve of that guy. It's not as if I had a lot of opportunity to get in trouble inside his apartment. The truth was, I had hoped that meeting up with Vincent would give me purpose. Instead, I only had a bunch of earthquake data to ponder. I'd traded in my parents' boring suburban home for the more picturesque tedium of having nothing to do on the Oregon Coast. Even as far as chasing windmills went, it lacked any real substance.

With no real idea what to do with my limited leads, I retreated to old habits of mindless channel surfing. For the better part of the morning, I shut off my brain, bouncing between game shows. Much as I loved the true crime genre, after my run-in with dude-bro, I opted for more light-hearted television.

It wasn't until I broke for a snack around 10 a.m., staring into the stark fridge of a single guy, that I confronted my own laziness. What was I doing? Was I waiting for Vincent to come home? Because his arrival wouldn't change anything.

I slumped onto the futon, now in couch form, the TV droning on in front of me. I'd become lost, rejected by shepherds due to my own hubris. Despite how critical they were of me and my lightning abilities, I now knew how much their world had meant to me. I might have been a wild card and didn't follow rules well, but we had purpose. Guntram had even given me hope that I could protect Nasci, like generations of shepherds before me.

But now he didn't believe in me. I'd finally broken one too many rules, and it had gotten someone killed. I wished I could make it right, but I couldn't. I could only verbalize what I wanted to say to Guntram.

"I'm sorry I disappointed you," I whispered to the empty living room. "Sorry everyone else was right about me, and you got screwed because you trusted me. It's my fault, Guntram, not yours."

It would have been easy to leave it at that and go back to watching TV, but somewhere outside, a storm brewed, tugging at my pithways. I cracked the blinds open and found the day had become overcast with dark rolling clouds. It probably wouldn't turn into a lightning storm because I couldn't feel that pith through the sheer humidity, but it reminded me of the fox dryant nevertheless. She'd reopened my pithways for a reason, and that reason wasn't to find out if some soccer Mom from Wisconsin would make it to the final round and win $30,000.

I shut off the TV, inhaled a stale granola bar and near-expired milk, and marched out of the gloomy apartment with my boots laced on.

Whenever Guntram and I had free time as shepherds, we always trained. Before the Rafe situation had literally blown up, we had been focusing on studying all four natural elements plus lightning. I'd already mastered water and fire skills, and ironically, had expanded my earth sigil repertoire when Rafe tried to bury me. With diminished pithways, though, I didn't know what I could do now.

I guess I'd have to test my skills and find out.

I headed for Clear Lake, a mile northeast of Vincent's apartment. Surrounded by sandy dunes to the west, the area did not permit ATVs, and the locals deemed the fishing prospects so-so. In other words, it was the perfect isolated spot for casting magic. I only had to cut through one block of residential homes before finding myself surrounded by trees. I made one detour around a gun club with firing ranges on the south end of the dunes. The sharp cracks of gunfire faded in the distance as I dove deeper into the forest.

I approached Clear Lake from the western sands, sticking to where conifers took root in the soil. I didn't need my fire pith for warmth as the overcast day heated up to a comfortable seventy degrees. A light breeze cooled my bare legs. I discarded my socks and footwear and let my toes sink into the muck at the edge of the lake—earth, air, and water pith cycling throughout my body.

I inhaled and exhaled. I planned to start small and work my way up. Spreading my legs apart in a sigil stance, I drew an airy sideways S, the wind whipping around my fingertips at my command. After a few minutes of that, I switched to square shapes, absorbing heavy earth pith and flinging sand. I ended up with a little sand in my eyes, but still, success. Water came next, stacking Vs on top of each other to divide the lake in front of me, revealing irritated crabs scuttling for cover. Finally, I expended fire pith by drawing a cross with long vertical line. My mood flickered as radiant as my fingerflames.

So far, so good.

With the tutorial out of the way, I focused on more advanced techniques. I recharged my pithways, letting all the natural elements flow over me. I'd passed the first bar with such ease, maybe I'd sail over the next hurdle as smoothly. I might even get some lightning practice in with the batteries in my kangaroo pouch.

No such luck.

You know how old cars protest when you try to

start them in the winter? My inner pith acted like that as I entered the second round, not hurting exactly, but creaking to ignite. I frowned in irritation over how long it took to refill my pithways to their maximum capacity, given the minor sigils I'd drawn.

Gazing out over the quiet lake, I decided to try walking on water. The lake's surface barely rippled, meaning I wouldn't even have to balance over rolling water. I strode into the shoreline. Water absorbed and pooled into the soles of my feet. My legs shook a little, but I chalked it up to nerves. Then, drawing a triangle over a series of waves, I stepped upward with a thrust meant to hoist myself on top of the water.

Instead of walking on the surface, though, my foot penetrated straight through. Off-balance, I tumbled face first into the lake.

Spitting, I crawled out of the lake, all my clothes soaked. In angry instinct, I drew a drying sigil. It should have flung all the water off me and made me dry.

It didn't. The water in my pithways lurched, and a small spray shot out of my bare arms, but my hoodie and shorts remained sopping wet.

"You've got to be kidding me." I'd mastered the drying sigil years ago. I tried it several more times, but my water pith refused to budge.

Breaths coming in ragged, I refused to give up. Maybe it was just water pith. I focused on my air pith, drawing two Ss for an infinity symbol that

DM FIKE

should have created a barrier of wind around me. The breeze around me hiccupped a bit, whipping hair into my face, but then died back down without much fanfare. Another failure.

Heart pounding now, I tried a few more moderate sigils: breaking a nearby boulder, creating a water stream from the lake, and sucking air into a mini-funnel. Nothing. Desperate, I reached into my pocket and pulled out the double A batteries I'd taken from home. Lightning was always erratic, but I could rely on it to pack a powerful punch. I drew a sigil of zigzags back and forth, pulling on the energy contained within the batteries to command a bolt of lightning.

Although I could feel a slight electric tingle, it was no use. My pithways refused to absorb the lightning.

I plopped down in the sand, astonished at how weak I'd become. I resisted the urge to chuck the stupid batteries out into the lake. Was this the extent of my abilities then? A handful of newb skills that I couldn't use to fight even the weakest vaettur?

I gave up on any further training. As I trudged back toward Vincent's apartment, I tried to focus on any bright side. At least the simple stuff worked fine. Maybe I needed more time for my pithways to heal. I drew a bit of inner fire to warm myself after the lake dunk, grateful that it helped dry me off even a little. Still, that bit of silver lining did nothing to dispel the metaphorical cloud hovering over my head.

Given my disappointment, I barely registered my surroundings, heading vaguely back in the direction I'd come. Out of habit, I kept mostly to the tree line, which ended up saving me. As I stepped behind a tree, gunfire cracked around me. Only then did I realize I'd wandered too close to the gun range. Squealing, I threw my hands over my face to protect myself as a branch collapsed down on me.

"Hold!" I heard someone yell. "Hey you! What are you doing here? This is private property!"

I fled back into the woods before any of the distant figures could get a good look at me. I heard someone pursuing me, but as I dove into thicker bramble, my pursuer couldn't follow. It was a small comfort that some of my abilities didn't require magic.

But that bullet whizzing by my head reminded me how much I'd relied on my pithways, not only to fight, but to keep me safe. I had no idea if what I had left would be enough to do any good.

CHAPTER 8

VINCENT BARGED INTO the apartment almost exactly after the microwave clock flipped over from 3:59 pm. The door bounced off the rubber door stop and saved his wall from damage. He glanced around suspiciously at the gloomy living room interior, disappointment already etched onto his face until he noticed me sitting on the futon, squinting uncomfortably at him.

My mouth twisted in a wry smile. "You thought I'd be gone, didn't you?"

"Of course not," he lied, throwing on a switch by the door. I groaned as the additional light pierced my eyeballs. "And why are you sitting in the dark?"

I didn't have the heart to tell him I'd been brooding over my lack of magical talent. "Just bored with TV."

"Well I got something to cure your boredom." He tossed a plastic see-through shell at me. I caught it, finding a prepaid cell phone strapped within. "I bought one for you during my shift. I even programmed it with my number."

I palmed it dubiously as he strode toward his

bedroom, already shrugging out of his uniform. "You think texting is going to solve my boredom?"

He shut his door, ostensibly to put on civilian clothes, so I didn't expect an answer. He shouted a muted response nevertheless. "Open the browser."

I did as requested, clicking around. Vincent had left a webpage open, the same USGS website he'd shown me at the bar with maps of red dots outlining quakes. "So? You already showed me this last night."

Vincent returned in a shirt and jeans, pushing the white pockets back into place near his hips. "Check out the point north of Noti."

Noti was a super small town between Florence and Eugene, less than an hour's drive away. Tucked in remote forests, I'd wisped past the area often when traveling from the homestead to the coast, viewing it from the mountains above but never having a reason to stop.

Pressing the red dot above Noti revealed details on a quake that had apparently happened in the middle of the night. 4.5 magnitude quake at a 0 km depth. I whistled at the stats.

"I know, right?" Vincent nodded. "I'm actually amazed we didn't feel it ourselves."

Me too but for a different reason. As a shepherd, I'd gotten used to faint natural tremors. Guntram had told me most of them occurred as Nasci herself shifted beneath the Earth's crust. I hadn't felt any since the battle on Mt. Hood, though, not even with my pithways restored. Yet another reason to get nervous about my current magical predicament.

"But there's more," Vincent continued. "Despite the readings, the geologists can't accurately locate the origin point. A magnitude of that size and depth should leave some marks on the surface, but their satellites couldn't find anything this morning."

I knew why that could happen. "The shepherds might be hiding it for some reason."

"My thoughts exactly. It's like trying to find your homestead. I'm sure the field guys are overlooking it disguised as a rock or something."

"But the shepherds would only cover something important to them." I chewed on the inside of my cheek. "I can't imagine what that would be."

"Well there's only one way to find out." He held his hand out to me. "Go see for ourselves."

I rubbed the back of my neck. "I'm not sure, Vincent. We have no idea what could be out there. And the other shepherds aren't too happy with me right now."

"Since when did that stop you? Besides, it's too close not to investigate. I don't have enough days off to go driving around the other earthquake sites on the other side of the state. This is our best bet."

He wasn't wrong. In a sea of stagnation, he'd found something actionable. It did me no good to chill in the apartment all day. "Fine, but you're buying dinner on the way."

He grabbed my wrist and pulled me upward.

"Deal."

* * *

True to his word, Vincent grabbed a greasy meal of burgers, fries, and root beer floats on the way out of town. We slurped as he navigated his car off the coast into the two-lane highway that fed back into the state. I fed him fries as the twisting roads forced him to use both hands to drive.

We passed by the river town of Mapleton. I recognized the bridge where I'd left a geezer once after saving him from his burning home. I realized with a pang that I'd never followed up on him.

"You don't happen to know a Mr. Pitts, do you?"

"The old farmer who likes to hunt without a license? Sure, I've met him. Really sucks that he lost his farm, though. It happened when..." His voice trailed off as he made the connection. "...you were hospitalized." A scowl marked his face. "That was Rafe too, wasn't it?"

"Yep." I sucked up the last dregs of my float.

Vincent's knuckles whitened as he strangled the steering wheel. "I really wish I could get my hands on that guy."

"Can't beat up a dead guy, much as we want to. But Mr. Pitts? Is he okay?"

"Yeah, don't worry about him. I hear he's living with his dog at his son-in-law's place, driving everyone crazy."

"Good to hear." I smiled at the image of anyone dealing with that old geezer on a daily basis. Maybe his dog Rufus would take the sting out of cohabitation.

Vincent glanced sideways at me. "You really care about him?"

"Care's a strong word. I used his barn as a place to store some extra cash. A little shepherd safe deposit box if you will, for a rainy day."

Vincent chuckled, shaking his head. "Ina, only you would do something as psycho as trespass on Pitts's property. I'm surprised he didn't use you for target practice."

"Who says he didn't?"

His chuckle erupted into full-blown laughter.

The rest of our conversation embodied the same light tone. We chatted about a number of inconsequential topics that flowed from one to another—whether we liked gingerbread after passing a restaurant themed in that vein, why I didn't consider myself a 'witch' (I threatened violence if he ever called me a hag), and the odd career path of game wardens in Oregon. The casual banter made me temporarily forget my worries, turning us into two ordinary people for a change. I didn't even mind when we got stuck behind an eighteen-wheeler going ten miles under the speed limit.

I wished we could preserve the moment forever.

A looming sign for Noti, though, eventually altered the mood. Vincent scooted forward in his seat, anticipating the exit.

"We need to take a left turn before entering town," he said. "Look out for a sign marking a tree farm."

We almost missed it since the dilapidated sign had been sun-bleached by years. Vincent had to execute a sharp turn to steer his Subaru onto an ill-maintained dirt path, heading into thick wooded forests with infrequent residential driveways. We bumped along until Vincent pulled over onto a relatively flat patch of weeds.

The smell of wet pine lit up my nostrils as we exited the car. Vincent ushered me toward a broad expanse of trees, a cool draft blanketing us as the surrounding vegetation blocked out the sun. After we lost sight of his car, he pulled out his phone and held it up for a signal.

I snorted. "As if that's going to work."

He waited a few beats before smiling, showing me an uploading map. "Ha! It does, actually. This is my work phone, and it's tapped into a satellite network not accessible by the public."

I threw up my hands in surrender. "I stand corrected."

Vincent shifted directions slightly based on his map. I couldn't tell where we were going. We'd moved so far away from the road that when an airplane passed overhead, it sounded as loud as a bullhorn.

As the noise faded back into silence, I asked, "What are you searching for?"

"I hoped you would know. Everything's going to appear normal to me, but we should approach the quake's epicenter very soon."

It's hard to find something that resembles everything else surrounding it. I used to cross the threshold of Sipho's homestead without sensing the magic that kept it hidden from outsiders. It wasn't until Vincent veered sharply to the side for no visible reason that I realized he had hit a barrier.

"Stop," I called to him. When he halted, I cut a straight line to the place he'd avoided. He flinched in surprise after I'd taken only a few steps.

"Hey!" He looked over my shoulder even though we were standing only yard apart. "Where'd you go?"

I walked back to him, his eyes scanning in my general direction. He couldn't see me until I came back within feet of his position. From his perspective, I must have popped out of nowhere because he sucked in a sharp breath of surprise.

"Boo!"

He ignored my childish proclamation and patted his hands against an invisible wall. "I guess you don't see the overgrown cedar trees here?"

I glanced around, but besides Douglas firs and ponderosa pine, I saw no red wooded bark.

"Nope. It's the barrier."

Vincent groped around the invisible trunk of a cedar. "Wow. Even the texture feels normal. That's incredible."

I glanced farther into the woods, past the line where Vincent could not cross. "You think the epicenter's back in there."

"A half mile at most, if the data is accurate."

I straightened my shoulders. "I'll go check it out."

"Wait." Vincent grabbed my sleeve before I vanished again. "You okay to go in alone?"

"Aren't you're the one who wanted me to do this? Well, now we're here, and I'm the only one who can go through. What else can we do?"

He reluctantly let me go. "Fine. I'm not budging from this spot, though. Just go in, check it out, and come right back out. And please"—his eyes darkened—"please don't get in any trouble. I can't help you from here."

I nodded, then moved forward.

As Vincent disappeared in the brush behind me, I upped my stealth game, careful not to crunch the brush underfoot. I crossed Mill Valley Creek, leaping on narrow stones, then treaded deeper into the forest. I hadn't made it very far when a sharp caw rang out above me. Blood pounding in my veins, I crouched down near a bush, hoping to pinpoint the bird. A flash of sable revealed a raven gliding through the canopy alone. He flapped once, twice, then faded into the leaves.

I swallowed. He could be a normal bird but probably not. Guntram had a special connection with ravens as kidama. They flocked to his bidding, both near and far, which made them an ideal spy network.

I followed discreetly in the bird's wake. As a kidama, the raven might scan the area for intruders. That meant the shepherds were indeed protecting something precious up ahead.

As I crept forward, I mentally prepared myself for coming face-to-face with my old augur. He'd decimate me in a fight, so I couldn't confront him. Staying low to the ground, I inched my way through the thicket, clutching to trunks and keeping my ears peeled for any sound. My caution paid off when a string of coughs sounded close ahead. A fiery glow lit up the shade, revealing a shadowy figure. I flattened myself against a tree, muscles tensed to flee.

"Man," a nasally voice managed between rasps. "Wish I could be in the hot spring right now."

I recognized Zibel, a coastal shepherd a rank above me. Zibel had been injured during the fight on Mt. Hood. When I'd sneaked off the homestead, he'd been among the unconscious healing from the ordeal. I guess this meant he'd recovered enough to handle normal duties.

I squatted low to the tree's roots, crawling for a better vantage. Through stalks of wildflowers, the forest opened up into an unnatural clearcut site. It might have been the staging area for a new forestry project. In the middle of that stark flat land, Zibel's red hair contrasted with the brown and green tones around him. He sat on a large boulder, overlooking a long, narrow pit. Freckles spattered his pale skin. He turned in profile, revealing bags under his eyes. Always jittery, his gangly knee bounced up and down, unable to sit still even for a moment.

The thing that really bothered me though, was the strange glow emitting from within the pit. It flickered at Zibel's feet, deeper in the ground than I could view at this angle. Why would Zibel build a fire if he could draw a sigil for warmth?

Zibel tilted his head toward me and said, "Glad you could keep me company at least."

I froze, thinking I was doomed until the raven swooped out of the sky and landed on the shepherd's shoulder. Zibel patted him on the head. "Only an hour until shift change. We're almost there."

He lapsed into silence, stifling yawns as the raven preened his feathers. A shift change? That meant shepherds had set up a watch system over whatever glowed in that strange pit. Guntram must have paired Zibel up with a raven as a precaution. The shepherds must have been spread pretty thin to send someone as bone-tired as Zibel to perform major guard duty with a kidama.

I itched to take a closer peek, but Zibel didn't seem intent on moving anytime soon. Ten minutes passed, and he continued to fidget in place, the raven content to perch on him. My legs cramped in such an awkward crouching position.

It occurred to me if I waited too long for a shift change, I might have to deal with not one but two shepherds. That probably wouldn't go well. My mind reeled for another solution when the sound of gurgling water entered my ears. Even though I'd crossed Mill Valley Creek, its tributary burbled somewhere to my right, curving around the field's border in a 'C' shape. Beyond Zibel, water glimmered in the foliage.

Pooling all my water pith, I lifted one hand and drew a simple V. I wanted to splash the water around enough for Zibel and his feathery friend to investigate. My first attempt, though, failed. The sigil, although simple, eluded my pitiful abilities.

C'mon, I thought, regathering what little water pith I had. Just reach, will you?

A second sigil released a shockwave from my hand. I steadied myself from falling as it shot across the clearing. It sounded like a large animal crashed through the creek. Zibel whipped around as the raven flew up into the air. The pair scampered away from me as they headed toward the racket.

Now was my chance. I bounded forward to where Zibel had been sitting only moments ago.

The pit wasn't manmade as I expected but a jagged crevasse of earth, like a mini canyon twenty feet in length by five feet wide. It cut ten feet deep, revealing a pool of magma not unlike the ones that haunted my dreams. The lava boiled like thick gravy, an occasional bubble popping. It cast a fiery gleam all around the enclave, giving everything a hellish tinge.

Someone had carved a direct wound straight into Nasci's earth, exposing her lifeblood.

A shuffling of ferns warned me of the pair's return. Sending out a second light wind gust, I swayed pine branches to mask my escape. I kept glancing over my shoulder for any sign of Zibel or the raven but didn't see either as I recrossed Mill Creek.

I must have passed Vincent at some point because he appeared out of nowhere to jog alongside me. "Hey! What did you find?"

"Sh!" I hissed back at him. "Get back to the car. I'll explain when we get there."

My warning came too late.

A sharp caw rang out above us. The raven screeched out a signal to Zibel as it dive-bombed us, all claws and fury.

I drew a sideways S and blew him out of the way before he hit Vincent. I cursed. Guntram would now definitely know I'd been here.

Vincent's Subaru came into view, and we crammed into it with record speed. Vincent had just started the ignition when a sudden shaking rocked the vehicle.

"INA!"

Peering in the sideview mirror, I saw Zibel emerge from the woods drawing squares, the dirt crumbling below him as he sent a quake straight toward the car.

"Go!" I yelled, an unnecessary command as Vincent floored the gas. The car lurched forward with a whiplash.

We bumped up and over a series of cracks in the road. In the end, a car is way faster than a shepherd and a raven. As we hit the main road and accelerated back onto the main highway, the trembling stopped. Zibel could not follow us.

Vincent kept scanning his rearview mirror as if expecting a ghost. "Who was that?"

I gritted my teeth. "That was a shepherd guarding Nasci's lifeblood. He now believes I tried to steal some, just like Rafe."

CHAPTER 9

VINCENT GRILLED ME on the way back to Florence, shattering our previous road trip vibe. What exactly had I seen? Why did Zibel guard it? What connection did it have to the uptick in earthquakes? My answers came out curt thanks to not having any answers. I could have kept my irritation to a manageable level, except Vincent decided to ruin it by taking things too far.

"That punk really tried to hurt us. Maybe shepherds aren't such pacifists after all."

Fire pith flushed my face. "I already told you, shepherds don't hurt people."

"Except you, and by proxy, me," Vincent said.

"I'm a loose cannon." I hated defending the shepherds' view of me but needed to get it through his thick skull. "Binding me is at the top of their to-do list, remember?"

"You're the one who pointed out the flaw with the random sneaker wave killing the Wonderland exec." Vincent's lips formed a grim line. "Shepherds are sworn to protect nature, right? Maybe they really are after Wonderland in the same way they're after you."

My composure snapped. "When did you suddenly became an expert on shepherds?"

He scowled. "I'm not, but I deal with facts and reason. And usually the simplest solution is the correct one. If the shepherds are hiding these earthquakes, and these earthquakes happened around the same time that Wonderland started experiencing unbelievable bad luck, maybe they're all connected."

I wanted desperately to argue with him, but the truth was, I had no idea what to think of that crevasse. It didn't resemble any lava dome I'd ever guarded. And it really did appear as if someone had torn open the earth using magic. The only people who could do that were shepherds. But why? My only innocent guess would be some sort of strange vaettur attack but even that seemed like a stretch.

So instead of a rebuttal, I went for an insult. "You want simple truth? You're just a regular dude dealing with forces you don't understand. Maybe your limited logic doesn't apply here."

A tick formed on Vincent's forehead. He opened his mouth but nothing came out. After miles of awkward silence, he flipped on the radio to a Latin music station. We both simmered, the upbeat music creating a contradiction to our dour moods.

We returned to the apartment around sunset. He retreated to his room, using an early shift the next morning as an excuse to go to bed early. I heard him shuffling around for a while. I buried the urge to knock on the door and attempt a reconciliation. Let him stew. The wound to my pride was too fresh to apologize. Instead, I made buttered toast and watched enough TV to realize I didn't care before turning in myself.

* * *

Despite broken sleep, I missed seeing Vincent get up and leave like I had the day before. With a new day underway, I felt awful about acting like a spoiled brat in the car. Without him, I would have never known about the lava crevasse in the first place. He'd been willing to share information since the beginning, and I'd responded with petty sarcasm. I promised myself I'd make things right when he came back.

Vincent aside, I had other things to worry about, like earthquakes, lava crevasses, and Wonderland Resorts. I had no idea how they all fit together, if they were even supposed to. While I didn't have a lot of options, I could check out Heceta Beach. Sure, it was a bit morbid to take a stroll where Borden had drowned, but maybe it would give me insight into this mess. Besides, the walk might alleviate my oncoming headache.

Exiting the apartment with purpose, I almost didn't catch the raven loitering in the parking lot. For a moment, I paused. This one seemed more interested in pecking the ground than screeching at me. I sauntered past her toward the trees, the bird not sparing me even a side glance. I guess that meant Guntram hadn't sent her.

At least the weather acted like full-blown summer for a change. The sun broke through the clouds, heating up the wooded area north of Vincent's apartment. I purposely avoided going anywhere near the gun club, not chancing a stray bullet to the brain. The meandering path added an extra ten minutes to my trip, but I used the time to refresh all four elements in my pithways. Before long, I spotted the twinkling blue lights of a wisp channel glowing at the base of a Sitka spruce. I dove in, expecting a splash of salty breeze on the other side.

Instead, smoke stung my nostrils.

I followed my nose toward the source of the haze, racing through a grove and emerging not far from a cul-de-sac of mansions, the literal end of Florence's residential roads. Built right next to the beach, all four structures were so huge and with such ample parking, at first I thought they were upscale condos. You had to have some serious dinero to own one of these babies.

And one of them was on fire.

The house in question looked somewhat like a layer cake, with a white rock façade encompassing the ground floor, yellow siding for the second floor, and red paint on the third. The expensive two-door entrance had exploded, bits of charred wood hanging from the doorway like broken teeth. Smoke billowed from the entry point, but the two upper floors leaked a much thinner gray mist. The surrounding yard was under some sort of land-scaping rehaul with flat dirt and piles of mulch adding to the starkness of the scene. Flames flickered here and there behind the windows, not yet penetrating the roof or walls.

Even more surreal than the house fire itself was the lack of activity around it. Nothing stirred—not a billowing curtain, cracked door, or peering face. I guessed everyone else had left for the day.

I pulled out the cell phone Vincent had given me and dialed 9-1-1. An operator immediately asked me why I'd called.

"Fire," I managed.

"What do you mean 'fire,' ma'am? A fire at your home?"

I shook my head like an idiot. Of course, she couldn't see me. "No, someone else's."

"Okay, what's the address?"

Address. I glanced around and saw plenty of house numbers but no street signs. When the operator pressed me again, I said, "I'm not sure. Northern most edge of town along the beach."

"Which beach, ma'am?"

"Heceta."

A shrill howl suddenly cut through the air. Glancing up, I spied the edge of a third-story balcony toward the mansion's left side. A flat-faced cat with long hair poked his head between the wooden rails and mewed. Soot spattered his fine white coat. The poor boy coughed between pleas for help.

DM FIKE

"There's a cat!" I yelled into the phone.

"You see a pet in the fire?" the operator asked.

"Yes!" I ran closer to get a better view of the kitty. He had exited from the sliding glass doors high above. Smoke slid out from within, trapping him on the balcony. "He's trapped!"

"Ma'am, stay on the line and answer my questions. Is anyone inside the home?"

Was she deaf or simply stupid? "I just said there's a cat."

"I mean people. I want to know if any people are inside."

The dismissiveness in her tone made my jaw clench. "The cat's life is enough."

I didn't give her a chance to respond. I ended the call.

I rushed toward the house, evaluating all my options. Directly beneath the cat on the ground floor were sliding glass doors on a wooden deck. Flames roared inside, enveloping all the furniture like Satan's living room. I couldn't enter there.

The second story had a balcony that ran the entire length of the house. I considered briefly casting focused air underneath my feet to "fly" upward but ditched that idea. I couldn't even pull off that kind of magic before with my normal pithways.

That left one last option: the rock façade comprising the first floor's exterior.

I pressed my hands up against the rock, gauging how much actual earth pith it contained. Processed materials often lose their natural energy, but these stones retained a decent amount of their original composition. I couldn't climb all the way up to the third floor, but I could get to the second story balcony. Gathering earth pith into my palms, I drew a square with a triangle and willed my hands to stick to the rocks' rough surfaces.

To my relief, my palms did attach. It wasn't an optimal adhesion, kind of like trying to climb over wet tide pool rocks. It would have to do. I painstakingly pushed upward, clinging to earth pith on the wall while my boot tips wedged between cracks for support. I slipped once, cutting my arm on a sharp edge, but didn't stop. Finally, I grasped the second-story balcony and pulled myself over the railing.

Long, hardwood planks stretched from corner to corner, providing a balcony to two different sets of smoky glass doors. I ignored the first one and ran to the opposite end. There, I could hear the cat yowling above the ceiling, which served as his floor.

"I'm here, kitty!" I yelled. "Just give me a second."

I couldn't stick to the siding. I needed a physical way to lift myself up. Glancing around, I found solid wood patio furniture. I pulled a single chair over to the side and used it as a step stool to stand on the balcony's railing. I tilted precariously on my tiptoes, the edge of the dirt lawn below giving me mild vertigo. Ignoring my fear, I planted one hand on the wall and reached above with the other to the third-story balcony. If I really stretched, I could grip the edge, but I didn't have the strength to pull myself up to grab the cat.

He'd have to come to me.

"Here, kitty!" I yelled, wriggling my fingers.

I barely felt the surge of fire in time. I wrote a quick cross with a pentagon as a flash of flames shot out from the third story's sliding glass doors. I thanked my quick thinking when my fingers cut through flame unharmed.

But that didn't help me rescue the cat. I heard him shuffle toward me and mewl, not daring to step closer to the fire.

I had to douse the flames. I gathered all my water pith and drew a long line of Vs, then finished it off with three lines bursting over the top. Water sprayed upward from my fingertips, and I directed it toward the sliding glass doors. I produced a lot less water than I intended, but it did the trick, creating steam out of the blaze.

When I ran out of water pith, I waved again at the cat. "Come here, kitty!" I encouraged.

I heard him padding around, but he continued to whine, not brave enough to come forward.

"I know it's tough," I cooed at him, hoping I had sufficient animal charisma to coax him. "I wouldn't want to do it either, but it's the only way out of here."

Seconds passed with no movement. I kept my fingers elongated toward him. I thought for sure he wouldn't come when fur suddenly became entangled in my palm.

"Good boy!" I yelled up at him. "Move around so I can grab your collar!"

The fur shifted until my knuckles scraped against hard leather. I got a firm grip on the collar, then gently pulled him through the rail posts down toward me.

I had to let go of the exterior wall so I could catch his body with my other arm, and for a split second, I leaned the wrong way toward the lawn below. Blasting wind to correct my unbalance, I landed on the second-story balcony with a thud, the cat cradled in my arms.

And just in time, too. A loud crack filled the air above us, sending a shower of glass falling like snow. A steady roar of flames sounded up above as ash floated down in its wake.

I shivered. "Whew! That was close. Let's get out of here, ok?"

But no sooner had I taken a few steps than the glass doors next to me suddenly shot open. I gathered all my fire pith to my palms, expecting flames to explode toward us. Instead of fire, though, a pale middle-aged man stumbled out of the smoke in a bathrobe. Covered with a fine layer of soot, he had an awful gash on his forehead that dripped blood down to his chin. His bloodshot, unfocused eyes only added to his zombie aura.

A startled cry escaped my throat.

The cat had the opposite reaction. He jumped out of my grasp and dashed over to the man, intertwining himself around his legs affectionately.

The cat jolted the man out of his stupor. He finally registered my presence, a flash of terror replacing the dull glaze. He took a half step back into the house and screamed, "Don't hurt me!"

Swallowing my heebie-jeebies at his horror movie appearance, I held out my hands to calm him. "I'm not going to hurt you."

The man acted as if I'd threatened him with a knife. He cowered with his hands to protect his face. "Please don't kill me! I'll give in to your demands!"

I didn't answer as something heavy crashed inside the house, causing my ears to ring. The house groaned as if in protest. The balcony beneath our feet shifted ever so slightly.

We couldn't stand around and have a leisurely conversation. We had to leave. Now.

I left the sobbing man to search the area below for a way to jump down safely. I could probably drop with the cat okay, but I doubted the undead walker would survive the impact. Fortunately, a mulch pile lay not too far below us, stacked six feet high. I gathered earth pith and added more mulch from the lawn to the top of the pile, giving it extra cushion. I then pulled another chair to the railing as a second stool.

Satisfied with my work, I turned back to the zombie. "Is there anyone else in the house?"

He gaped at me. "What?"

I resisted shaking him, but my voice rose a few notches. "Is there anyone else inside? Your wife?

Another pet?

He shrank a little at my tone. "No."

"Then let's go!"

He whimpered as I grabbed him by the arm and led him toward the balcony's edge. He was surprisingly compliant in his panic, following me despite his many protests to the contrary. Even when I pulled him upward to stand on the chair, he did so without resistance.

"Jump!" I ordered, pointing down to my makeshift mulch cushion.

Tears streaked down his face, mixing with blood. "I'll do anything. I swear! Just leave me alone!"

The house shook again. I didn't have time for this. I gathered my air pith and sent him over the railing with a blast. I leaned over the railing as he fell, sending air blasts beneath him to slow his descent. My pithways recoiled in agony as I blew past my limit, but I refused to stop. The man screamed the entire descent, but he floated down more like a balloon than a rock and hit the mulch with barely a bounce.

I scooped the kitty back up in my arms. "I wish I had only saved you," I told him, then leaped over the side myself.

Right as my boots hit the ground, bits of both balconies creaked to warn of their loss of structural integrity. I pulled us away from the building toward the street as smoke and fire burst out of the doors. I'd just gotten the man to sit on the curb when an explosion rocked the house and that entire side of the house collapsed.

"Glad that wasn't close," I groaned, wiping black gunk from my face.

But I didn't have time to rest as a wall of sirens surged toward us. Two cop vehicles wound their way up the street in our direction.

I couldn't be connected to this fiery mess. "The police are coming," I told the man, placing his grateful cat into his lap. "Stay here."

I barely made it back into forest cover before the first black SUV arrived. It screeched to a halt not far from the zombie. I didn't dawdle around long enough for anyone to spot me. I fled the scene.

CHAPTER 10

I CRUMPLED INTO a ball on the other side of the wisp channel, on the verge of hyperventilating. The enormity of what had happened finally caught up to me. The cat, zombie man, and I could all have burnt to a crisp.

I hated rescue missions.

A buzzing jolted me out of my stupor. The cell phone in my hoodie pouch rang. I answered it with trembling fingers.

"Hello?"

Vincent didn't mince words on pleasantries. "Please tell me I didn't see you running back into the woods off Shoreline Drive?"

I didn't have the energy to lie. "That was your SUV?"

Vincent gave a muffled curse. Then he took a deep breath and commanded, "Go back to the apartment, Ina, and stay there."

My shoulders tightened. "Hey, don't get mad at me. I saved a cat's life. Oh, and some dude too."

Vincent growled into the phone. "Don't pretend Lee Foster doesn't have anything to do with this."

"Lee Foster?" That name sounded familiar, but my muddled brain couldn't place it.

"I knew shepherds were involved in all this." His loud voice sounded angrier than I'd ever heard him. "It's probably another secret you're hiding from me."

"What are you talking about?"

A flurry of sirens sounded on his end. "Do me a favor and chill back at the apartment. Don't run off, don't play hero, just do it. Now!"

Then he hung up on me.

I stared blankly at the phone. I cut off Vincent all the time. He never did the same to me.

That name. I opened the phone's browser and did a quick web search. The results that came back would have knocked me over if I hadn't already been sitting down.

Lee Foster, CEO of Wonderland Resorts. Several websites displayed his profile picture, so there was no mistaking the zombie from the house fire.

An earthquake had buried the Mt. Hood Wonderland resort. A sneaker wave had drowned the CFO. And now a house fire had almost killed the CEO.

"Dammit." I got to my feet, which instantly made me feel light-headed. I couldn't think with my pithways aching all over. I wished I had access to a hot spring, but I'd have to settle on a long, hot bath. I had no idea what was going on with Wonderland and the shepherds, but after everything that had gone down, I owed Vincent. I'd stay put for a change and wait for him to come back from work.

* * *

Four o'clock came and went. Then five, six, and seven. You can only pass so much time cooped up in an empty apartment before you lose your mind. No amount of bathing, napping, and channel surfing would calm me. I sent Vincent a couple of text messages asking when he'd return but never got an answer.

More than anything, I wanted to locate Vincent and untangle this awful mess. He probably thought I'd gone to Lee Foster's house as part of some secret shepherd mission. Earlier this year, I might have gotten angry at his assumption, but now I knew I deserved it. I'd kept too many secrets from too many people. The only chance I had to win back his trust was to explain the whole ridiculous mess and pray he'd believe me.

As Vincent's microwave clock approached eight, though, I about lost my nerve. Not knowing anything drove me up a wall. I almost left out of sheer nervous jitters when footsteps sounded outside on the walkway. I cued up everything I'd planned on saying to him about Foster's fire, prepared to battle to the bitter end for truth.

Vincent opened the door with slow resignation, which only changed to surprise when he caught me sitting ramrod straight on the edge of the futon.

"You're here?" he asked, a hint of surprise in his voice.

I nodded curtly, not sure how to reply without sounding defensive. He was the one who wouldn't answer my stupid texts.

"Oh," he said.

I waited for him to continue. He didn't. Instead, he slowly dragged his dirty body inside along with a laptop and a bag of fast food.

I expected him to justify his silence, given how angry he'd been on the phone. But when he offered me the laptop with a dejected look on his face, I didn't know what to do.

"What's this?"

"An apology. I never should have doubted you."

I recoiled in suspicion. "Why?"

"Just open it." When I still didn't take the laptop, he plunked it down on the dining table. He clicked around a bit and then swung the screen to face me. "I need a shower. That should give you time to get up to speed."

As he shuffled down the hallway, I yelled after him. "Aren't you curious how I ended up at Foster's?"

"I'm sure it's a good story," he called back, then shut the bathroom door. The sound of a shower filled the apartment.

He didn't want me to explain myself? The world had gone completely crazy. I slid into a chair at the table and adjusted the laptop screen to my height, dreading what would break Vincent so completely.

A still image popped out at me. It was Rafe walking up the driveway to Lee Foster's beach house, timestamped a half hour before I arrived. I'd forgotten how off-a-magazine-cover handsome he was with his wispy blond hair and finely-toned abs, visible underneath a taut athletic shirt. He must have realized he would be caught on film because he directed his striking blue eyes directly at the camera.

Right at me.

A gasp escaped my throat. I slammed the screen shut.

Even without him smirking at me, I stifled the urge to vomit. I'd seen him fall to his death on Mt. Hood. He couldn't have survived that. Tabitha had given her life so he wouldn't terrorize anyone else ever again. He couldn't just come back to life like a little cockroach.

And yet, his reappearance fit with the facts perfectly. Before he died, he'd been on a mission to destroy the Wonderland resort on Mt. Hood. He also had a history of murdering people he felt threatened Nasci. It made sense he would kill the top executives who'd made the decision to start the project in the first place.

My mind spun so much that I didn't even hear Vincent take a seat next to me. I jumped when he said quietly, "It wasn't your shepherd friends."

As my heart rate dropped, I answered. "But they must know he's back, otherwise they wouldn't guard those crevasses." I bit my lip to keep it from trembling. "They're protecting the lava from him."

"I had the same thought." Vincent reached over and snagged the laptop back. He clicked around a spreadsheet of seismologic data he'd created. "I cross referenced the recent earthquakes with anything connected to Wonderland Resorts. They seem to coincide, all happening within twenty-four hours of the destruction of the Mt. Hood resort, Borden's drowning, and now Foster's accident." He slumped a little over the table. "It can't be coincidence."

I dug my nails into my palms as the implications of Rafe's reappearance sent me reeling. "Tabitha failed. She must not have sealed the lava dome fully before Rafe fell into Darby's crater on Mt. Hood. Now he's absorbing magma directly from Nasci again. No wonder he can level whole construction sites with earthquakes and firebomb a mansion. He's got incredible power on his hands."

Vincent laid his hand on mine to stop me from drawing blood. "And you knew nothing about this when you found the fire at Foster's?"

I shook my head, telling him the whole story. He accepted everything at face value, a huge relief. I didn't have the emotional bandwidth to give any of my previous speeches.

"It makes sense," Vincent said. "Borden had been in town visiting Foster at his Heceta Beach home. Rafe must have been waiting for his opportunity to murder both of them."

"So, what now?" I stood. "How do we catch

Rafe?"

Vincent pointed to the fading light outside the window. "We're not finding him tonight. Rafe's a fugitive from law enforcement, remember? There's already a warrant out for him on an arson that predates all this stuff. The image from Foster's security system is enough for the state police to put out an APB. I asked the night patrol to call me if they hear anything about him."

Vincent's mention of the camera suddenly made me nervous. "And what about me? Are the police looking for me?"

Vincent flashed me a wry smile. "You, my friend, have the devil's luck. The fire melted the camera and most of its backup storage. We were lucky to even retrieve that one still shot. No one knows you were even there except Foster, and given his strange depiction of you appearing out of nowhere like 'a devil,' the detective in charge thinks you're a figment of Foster's PTSD."

Well, that was a relief at least. "Will an officer protect Foster at the hospital?"

Vincent snorted. "Not if Foster can help it. He's fighting to get discharged immediately and return home to Eugene. He doesn't feel safe in Florence."

I remembered the wild glaze in Foster's eyes. "He knows Rafe wants him dead."

Vincent nodded. "He's obviously not telling us everything. It's hard to say if Rafe confronted him directly or not, but Foster's head wound may have been an assault. Without Foster's cooperation, though, it's hard to move forward."

"Well, there has to be something we can do."

"We can eat." Vincent gestured to the now luke-warm food bag in front of us. "And get some rest. I have a hunch we're going to need it."

CHAPTER 11

"HAGGARD!"

Tabitha stood at the edge of a molten precipice, hands on her hips, the glow from the lava casting odd shadows over her face. She appeared even more menacing than when she'd been alive.

"Why did I even sacrifice myself?" she spat at me.

I held up my hands in defeat. "I'm sorry. I had no idea Rafe was alive."

"Don't just stand there." She straightened, and in doing so, somehow grew giant-sized. "Do something about it."

Then a huge spray of lava burst behind her like some awful tidal wave hitting the shore. It enveloped her, and when it sizzled back below, she had vanished.

My heart twisted, but I waited for the dream to end. To wake up.

But for some reason, it didn't. And worse, I felt someone watching me. I glanced around the barren landscape, all jagged black rocks and lava pits, spewing out bubbles at random intervals.

"Tabitha?" I called uncertainly.

A disembodied voice drifted up over the steam. It was so faint, I couldn't make out the words at first.

Jump in.

The monotone whisper repeated itself over and over, a broken sound bite set to infinite repeat.

An invisible force pushed me forward, right toward the ledge where Tabitha had stood. I tried to fight against it, but you can't hurt something you can't touch. I drew earth sigils to bind me to the ground, but my boots prevented skin contact. The force pushed me so fast I didn't have time to take them off. Digging in my heels didn't slow me either, despite my leverage.

Jump in. Jump in. Jump in.

I found myself teetering over a wide lake of roiling magma. Screaming, I arched my torso backward as much as possible, but it made no difference. The ground beneath my feet vanished, and I fell down, down, down toward the depths.

"Ina!"

Vincent's voice broke through the fog, and my real eyes opened. I flung myself upward, the top of my head bashing into Vincent's face. We yelped in unison.

Ache along my hairline receding, I shivered on Vincent's futon, covered in a light sweat. He sat on the floor beside me, fully dressed in his black officer uniform, rubbing his chin.

I tried to make sense of the dream. I'd never

grown used to the nightmares, but having one take off in such a strange, vivid direction really creeped me out. I'd felt completely awake and aware of my surroundings, from the macabre voice to the sensation of falling to the realization that I would die.

I inhaled and exhaled deep breaths to calm my frazzled nerves. "Sorry," I managed. "Nightmare."

Vincent grunted in response, an acknowledgement of my apology but not yet ready to accept it.

I glanced over at the microwave. 7:30 in the morning. "Maybe I wouldn't maim you if you didn't wake me up so stupid early."

Vincent pulled himself up to his feet. "Lee Foster is dead."

He might as well have slapped me across the face. "But I thought he was recovering in the hospital yesterday."

"He was. I got a call from my buddy on patrol. Seems Foster convinced the hospital to discharge him, but he died outside town on his way home. Apparently, there were unusually high winds on Highway 126 that knocked down a power pole and struck his BMW, killing him instantly."

My hand came to my mouth. "Rafe."

Vincent nodded grimly. "The OSP are labeling it an accident, but yeah, sure sounds like it." He grabbed his ranger hat, keys, and wallet off the counter.

"Are you going to check out the accident?" I asked as he approached the front door.

"Yeah." He paused with his hand on the doorknob. "Look," he said as I threw my hoodie over my borrowed T-shirt. "I know you want to come, but I can't take you. This is official police business. It's not like I have visitor badges for this kind of thing."

I crammed my feet into my boots. "You don't have to bring me right up to the accident. Drop me off nearby. I can watch from a distance."

"What if someone sees you?"

I tied the laces as fast as I could. "I could pretend to jog or something."

Vincent rolled his eyes. "In the middle of a highway? Wearing hiking boots?"

"Fine, a hike then." I sprang to my feet. "I'm sure I'll think of something."

Vincent opened the door but kept his back to the dawning sky. "You should stay here, Ina. You're safer here."

An ear-shattering caw interrupted further argument. That one sharp call set off a cacophony of raven screeches that probably woke up half the block.

Vincent and I both warily stepped outside and peered over the second story railing. Ravens blanketed the entire parking lot, a dot matrix printout of black overlaid over cars, painted lines, and bare concrete. Their heads all swiveled in our direction, and once they caught sight of me, they grew louder, an angry mob obviously finding their target.

Guntram's kidama. So that had been his raven

yesterday. I cupped my hands over my mouth to be heard over the din. "Here I am! You found me!"

Ebony feathers took to the air, a coordinated flock as they swooped high above me. Vincent grabbed my arm, intending to pull me back into the apartment, but I shook him off.

"Go on!" I screamed. "Tell Guntram I'm here!"

A few cackles later, and they did just that, bolting as one horrifying unit up into the sky. The sound of hundreds of wings flapping caused its own wind gust, no pith required. They flew like a biblical locust swarm as they took off toward the east, their caws slowly fading.

I turned back to a stunned Vincent. "Still think I'm safe here?"

Vincent adjusted the brim of his hat, which had fallen askance. "C'mon," he grumbled, waving a few of his neighbors away as they peeked out their windows to investigate the commotion. "Let's go."

* * *

Despite an ominous start, a beautiful Oregon day had already begun to blossom. Half the sky was lit up in brilliant pinks as a chilly, yet refreshing, humidity lingered. As we drove through town, a handful of RVs bumbled around the roads, heading toward adventure in remote areas. Once outside Florence, buildings gave way to the Siuslaw river on one side and a thick forest on the other. A magical summer morning.

I wished I could revel in it like I normally would.

Instead, I sat next to a tense Vincent as he drove away from the ocean. He gave me an extensive list of instructions. Things like, I'll drop you off a half mile away but keep your distance. Call me on the cell phone if you need to contact me. Don't get spotted by the other officers.

Meanwhile, my mind worried about what would happen after we inspected the wreck. I kept glancing upward for a feathery snitch, but no ravens trailed us. That didn't mean they weren't around.

Their arrival meant I couldn't stay at Vincent's apartment anymore. Guntram knew I'd be there. Shepherds hated traveling inside towns because it cut them off from their normal pith sources, but Guntram would make an exception in my case. I'd caused too much trouble, and he probably assumed I was working with Rafe again.

But I wasn't. I had to settle things with that bastard once and for all.

Vincent pulled off the side of the road next to an abandoned pier on the river. He pointed toward the rising sun. Squinting against the glare, I could just make out flashing lights, though not much else.

"That's Foster's BMW up there."

"Okay." I opened the passenger side door and scooted to hop out.

Vincent surprised me by grabbing me by the wrist. "You sure you'll be safe by yourself?"

"Of course." I flashed him my most confident

smile. I almost added 'like always,' but then realized that would freak him out even more.

Vincent gave me one last squeeze. "I'll call for your location and pick you up when I'm done. I'll try to be as quick as possible."

Instead of agreeing, I simply slammed the door shut. I didn't have the heart to confess that I might not be able to go back with him. I wished that I could tell him how much I appreciated everything he'd done for me, but that would tip him off. I swallowed a lump in my throat as he drove off into the sunrise.

Shaking my limbs of excess emotion, I assessed my surroundings. I'd traveled this way hundreds of times before, although usually not so close to the road. The river, unfortunately, had little brush coverage. If I approached from that side of the road, the cops would see me coming from a mile away. That left me with climbing the steep hills on the other side. Covered in blackberry bushes, mature birches, and Douglas firs, it afforded ample coverage for a better view of the accident.

My pulse calmed as I entered the relative safety of the woods. The shadows under the canopy took some of the sting out of the sun's rays. I absorbed earth, air, and water pith as I trudged up the incline, converting some of it into fire. My pithways felt full of sludge, which I hated, but at least I could pull some water out of the air to drink with a basic sigil. Making it halfway up the hill, I forged a path through the brush that paralleled the road.

Even through the dense foliage, I caught glimpses of cars rushing past on the highway every now and again.

I made it to a spot overlooking the wreckage, although trees partially obstructed the view. I eventually had to shimmy partway up a fir, wedging my butt between a branch and a trunk. I grumbled at the discomfort as I took full inventory of the awful scene.

The BMW's roof had caved into a terrible U-shape, marking where the pole had struck. Steel jutted over the driver's seat and slashed toward the back end of the car. A dark stain glistened near where they'd used the Jaws of Life to retrieve the body. I honestly couldn't tell if it was oil or blood. Glass lay shattered like confetti, accented by the strobing lights of police lights, a grim party of death to mark that pancake of a vehicle.

They really thought a freak wind did this? I licked my finger and raised my hand into the sky. Not a breeze rustled by. The leaves barely moved. It couldn't have been more hushed if we'd been sitting inside a dusty snow globe.

"Rafe," I had to get into this psychopath's head if I wanted to find him. I imagined his last 24 hours. First, he'd beaten me to Foster's house and lit the place on fire. Then he might have found out via the news that his assassination attempt had failed. From there, he could have waited outside the hospital until Foster was discharged and followed him until he had an opportunity to kill him.

Where would he go now? The wind gust that broke the power line required a decent amount of air pith to knock over. But between it and the fire, he probably needed to recharge. I grabbed the cell phone from my kangaroo pouch and flipped it open to the USGS website Vincent had bookmarked for me.

The map jumped out at me with all its measle-like dots spreading across Oregon. I played around with the parameters until I found a way to search all the earthquakes by date, then sorted them by most recent.

Just 25 miles down the road, not far from the Whittaker Creek Recreation Site, a 4.0 level earthquake had occurred within the last fifteen minutes.

I blanched. I really should have felt that quake, but perhaps Vincent's car had muted it from me. More important than that, though, I had a lead on Rafe.

Pushing Vincent's number, I scanned for him among the handful of emergency personnel milling about the accident. I found him in a heated debate with another officer near the wreckage. Vincent excused himself and answered on the third ring.

"Yeah?" He did not sound thrilled.

I forged ahead anyway. "There's been an earthquake down the road. How much you wanna bet it's Rafe?"

"That's great," he said in a flat tone.

Great? I frowned at him through the trees. "Don't you think we should check it out?"

"Sorry, I got called unexpectedly into work." He glanced over at the officer he'd been talking to, who had his arms folded impatiently as he waited for Vincent to get off the phone. "Maybe we could make plans for tonight?"

Wonderful. Vincent had been suckered into the classic "you're here, you might as well work" boss maneuver. I didn't have time to wait for his superiors to give him permission to leave. Rafe could be long gone by then.

"I'll check it out myself."

Vincent straightened, scanning across the road for me, although he never quite looked in my direction. "I'd rather we went together," he said with a strained face.

Neither of us could afford this argument. "I'll be careful," I promised. Then I hung up the phone.

Vincent's face scrunched up in frustration, but with a fellow officer watching his back, he mouthed "bye," then shoved the phone back into his pocket.

"Sorry," I whispered to him. Then my feet flew toward the nearest wisp channel.

CHAPTER 12

IT TOOK ME two wisp channels and ten minutes of sprinting to reach Whittaker Creek. It dawned on me as I ran that Rafe could have taken the same path to get there. I wished I had one of Sipho's defensive charms to protect me from an ambush, but I settled on redirecting pith toward rounded trapezoids over my torso and face. The defensive sigils tied up some of my already limited pith stores, but it was better than nothing.

The earthquake's epicenter lay south of the campground, far away from the service road. Most of the rolling hills held densely packed forests, until suddenly they did not. I found a bulldozed patch of woods, completely flat for yards around. A jagged crack of earth ran right down the center, a fiery glow emitting from within.

I inhaled a breath. Everything looked eerily similar to the crevasse at Noti. This had to be where Rafe had gone.

I stayed within the tree line, waiting for him to appear. Nothing. I almost expected another shepherd or at least one of Guntram's ravens to make an entrance but still nothing. In fact, besides the occasional gurgle of lava, the place stayed unnaturally quiet, not even animals scurrying under the sunshine.

Vulnerable like Bambi's mother, I tiptoed out into the open. Crossing the distance to peer down into the chasm, I shivered as I contemplated the taffy-like ropes boiling below. Tabitha had jumped into that flesh-dissolving goo to seal Nasci away from Rafe. She gave her life. And yet, it hadn't worked.

"How can I do this if she couldn't?" I asked the lava.

As if in response, Rafe's face seemed to float underneath the lava. He appeared peaceful, eyes closed, mouth relaxed. At first, I thought it a trick of my overactive imagination, but then his head bobbed up above the surface, thin sheets of red-hot magma falling off him like jelly. He exhaled a gulping gasp, eyes bursting open. A sudden biting wind was my only warning of the upcoming explosion, but it convinced me to scramble backward just before the lava shot skyward like a geyser. The earth trembled beneath my boots as I crab-walked away from the resulting splatter.

As graceful (and naked) as Aphrodite waltzing from the sea, Rafe strode forward, planting both feet on the ground before me. I refused to look down at his junk, focusing on his face. Not a hair on his head stood out of place. An angry scowl formed on his lips.

"You," he sneered, executing a rapid-fire set of air sigils. Hurricane gusts swirled around me, rocking me back and forth until they lifted me up off the ground. My cries became lost to the wind as I flailed to find any solid thing to grab but found none.

Rafe held me aloft effortlessly, an astounding feat given that I'd only ever seen Guntram execute this sigil, and he's an expert at air pith. My fingers wriggled about desperately to come up with a counter wind, but my pitiful pithways didn't have the energy to counteract that level of magic.

Rafe noticed my failure and smirked. "Having trouble, legendary lightning shepherd?"

"You murdering coward!" I yelled back at him.

Rafe cocked his head. "Have you been following me? Is that why Foster survived the fire?"

I wanted to slap his smarmy little face. "Someone has to stop you!"

"It won't be you, not after what you did to your pithways absorbing all that vaettur energy." Rafe made a tsking noise. "You really should be more selective about whom you trust, Ina."

I pooled every last ounce of pith I could into my fingertips. "If not me, the other shepherds will find you. They won't let you absorb Nasci's lifeblood and continue your little crime spree."

"What can they do?" Rafe barked back. "Even the high and mighty Tabitha believed she could close the lava dome, but she failed. I managed to not only survive my fall into the earth but to locate a magma vein and claw my way out." He threw out his hands, and flames leaped from his palms with barely a sigil stroke. "And now I can feel Nasci's lifeblood everywhere. I can hear her whispers underneath the surface of the earth and create my own wounds directly into her flesh."

I stiffened with dread as I realized the true implications of this confession. Rafe himself had dug these awful crevasses. "You can't do that!"

"Why? Because Guntram told me not to?" He snapped out a bitter chuckle. "I tire of working in the shadows. It's time to show people what real shepherds are capable of. And once I'm finished with Wonderland, Guntram and the rest of the Talol Wilds are next on my list."

As Rafe lost the sanity in his expression, my fingers went through all the sigils I hoped to execute. A fireball. A water blast. I even tried absorbing the double A batteries in my kangaroo pouch. Every attempt fizzled out. I didn't have the ability to do a damn thing.

Rafe drew Ss in the air. "I don't know if your pithways will ever heal again, but I'm not going to let you find out. You've caused enough trouble as is."

He jerked his hands toward the lava crevasse. The obeying winds flung me over. I clawed around like a cat stuck in a burlap sack, my movements about as effective. My heart pounded as I hovered over the lava pit as it threatened to melt me into nothingness like Tabitha.

"Rafe!" I tried one last plea, not above a bald-faced lie. "I could show you lightning pith."

He shook his head. "I'm sorry, Ina. You're too much of a liability. Goodbye."

Then he released the wind, and my body hit the lava. For a brief moment, energy lit up my pithways in a pulsating strobe. I could taste fire, see air, smell water, and hear earth. My senses reached out into the surrounding Oregon wilderness, past the Pacific Ocean, and out across every country thousands of miles away. If a pebble toppled off a cliff in India, I could have grabbed it with my palm.

I might have become Nasci herself.

Then the moment passed. My flesh vaporized as I sunk below the coils. Thankfully, my nervous system shut down before I could comprehend the horror of such an ugly death.

CHAPTER 13

IT'S DIFFICULT TO describe what happened next since technically I didn't exist anymore. Lava doesn't tend to leave a recognizable corpse behind. Despite this physical setback, my pithways stayed intact. I could still manipulate all the elements: earth, fire, air, and water. I could even swish them around a little, like shaking an almost empty milk jug, though I didn't have hands to cast any magic.

My consciousness seemed fine too. I could string a litany of curses at Rafe no problem, the strong desire to wring his neck not abating even a little. As I sank deeper and deeper into a colorless, sensationless world, that rage morphed into sadness. I'd never hug my parents again. Never make it up to Guntram. Vincent would never know what happened to me, since I'd disappeared off the face of the planet.

Dammit, I thought, unable to cry tears. This sucks.

"Life sucks, haggard. You better get used to it."

I didn't have any body parts to move, but I wanted to turn toward that familiar voice. Tabitha?

I didn't see her, per se, but she appeared anyway, an entity made up of pith, mostly rock-solid earth with heapings of the other three elements as well. What she lacked in physical form, she made up with her usual attitude.

"Don't ask stupid questions. Who else would you expect to meet inside Nasci's lifeblood?"

Tabitha could read my mind. Interesting.

I don't know, I thought. Maybe Nasci herself.

Tabitha groaned. Apparently, she could still do that. "That's just like you, haggard, thinking the goddess will come personally greet you whenever you come calling."

Well, I am dead. Aren't I supposed to get re-absorbed back into her or something?

"Normally that's true. But as usual"—Tabitha somehow audibly executed an eye roll—

"you get to be the exception to the rule."

Exception?

"Don't let this get to your head, Miss Lightning Shepherd. You messed up big time up there."

You mean Rafe?

"Of course, I mean, Rafe!" My (inner?) pith swirled a little, sensitive to Tabitha's irritation. "Are you paying attention to his body count at all?"

An intense guilt washed over me.

Tabitha, I'm sorry. It's my fault.

"Your fault?" Tabitha snapped. "Are you trying to say I died because of you?"

Well, yeah, I did help Rafe.

She yanked nearly all the pith out of my pithways, an action that left me disoriented. "Are you saying I don't have any free will of my own?"

Well, no but—

"Then don't try to act like you control everything in the entire universe. I'm a shepherd, just like you. I protect Nasci. It's what I do. And no one tells me how to do it."

So, you're not angry with me?

"Yes, I'm angry with you." She absorbed all of my earth pith, paradoxically lightening my intangible form. "Can't you feel I'm angry?"

Yes. Definitely.

Tabitha sighed. "Let's get this over with."

Get what over with?

But instead of a reply, a bolt of lightning hit my pithways, zipping up and down. I swear I could pinpoint each individual atom it touched. My pithways twisted inside out like someone wringing a towel dry, an unnatural bending of everything that remained of me. This pushed me past my bearable pain threshold. My consciousness flickered but did not succumb. I held onto one thought, screaming out in my mind for mercy.

Tabitha!

"Quit whining and hold on." Her voice held a bitter, strained edge.

The pressure intensified for one last second, then eased. The wringing lessened, flattening me back out. I felt more solid, but light, floating away. I knew, despite having no real senses, that I drifted away from Tabitha.

Wait! Tabitha, what's going on?

Her voice grew fainter. "Rafe's weak now, but his power will grow if left unchecked. You still owe me, haggard. Prove me wrong."

Then an intense light overwhelmed me, and I became disoriented once again.

CHAPTER 14

THE LIGHT SEARED my skull. I didn't recognize it at first, having gotten used to not having a skull at all. Or eyes for that matter. It's a good thing shepherds bend the rules of nature because I only became aware that I'd been staring up in a daze at the sun after an incredibly long time. Any other person would have been blinded.

My cheeks grazed wet grass. It tickled my bare back. My limbs creaked to life like a junkyard car, leaden and rusty. The breeze brought the scent of a nearby cedar grove. My heat sensitivity returned, and good thing too, because as I turned over to one side, the radiating warmth of the lava crevasse warned me right before I might have plunged back into the magma itself.

I gave out a half-strangled cry as I rolled away from a second trip to death. Panting, I stared down at my naked knees, which rose up to my exposed thighs and continued all the way up to my bare chest.

I didn't have a stitch of clothing on me.

A blush spread over my face despite being all

alone in the middle of nowhere. I backed away from the crevasse and tried to ascertain facts. Rafe had thrown me into the lava, but instead of dying, I'd been dumped unharmed back into the forest. I could only conclude the weird encounter with Tabitha hadn't been a dream but the real deal. She'd saved me from evaporating and brought back my physical form. It made sense that, like Rafe before, she couldn't bring back my clothes.

But why?

My bare feet slid in a patch of earth, reflexively absorbing earth pith. I didn't expect the surge that flooded through my pithways. More rushed in than if I'd opened a dam. I staggered for a second, wondering how I could handle so much pith.

And that's when it hit me. I raised a hand up into the air to catch the breeze. Instead, the gentle wind whistled as it entered the huge empty cavities inside myself.

My pithways had been restored to their pre-Rafe status.

Jittery with glee, I followed the sound of rushing water back to Whittaker Creek. I ignored the jabs under my soles, for once not caring that I didn't have boots. When I got to the water's edge, I took a deep breath. Even at its most calm spot, the creek ebbed and flowed due to the rocks and shallow depths. Walking on water here would be much more difficult than a lake.

But I had to try.

Plunging both hands into the creek, I whipped

up fire pith to keep my bare butt warm. I also absorbed ample water pith for my next move. Then, with babbling pith flowing through my veins, I drew a triangle over a series of waves and took a step forward.

My foot landed squarely on the water's surface as if it were made of stone.

Giggling, I took another step. There was no doubt about it. I had the ability to walk up and down the creek, no problem.

I jumped back to shore and tested out a few more sigils. I located a gigantic boulder and tossed it across the creek with ease. I flung wind around me, wrapping my nakedness in a flurry of movement like satin bedsheets. I could even maintain a decent fire stream from one hand, aiming it down at the water where it sizzled into a steamy fog that billowed around my calves. I gave out a primal scream of joy.

My magic had returned.

As the echoes of my elation faded, I realized I now had a fighting chance against Rafe. Even he couldn't manipulate lightning. I couldn't wait to get my hands on some batteries so I could fry his smug smile right off.

But as goosebumps formed up and down my exposed flesh, I had other immediate worries. I couldn't waltz back into Florence looking like this. I needed clothes, and the nearby campground might have some I could "borrow."

I picked my way through the woods, treading

directly on small rocks and twigs. I softened the prickly sensation by extending earth pith into my feet. It made them feel heavy but created a cushion that lessened most of the impact.

The Whittaker Creek Recreation Site was pretty quiet when I arrived. Most campers had already left to enjoy the Siuslaw's beauty, leaving their belongings scattered around tents. I surveyed several campsites before I found one with a large 6-person tent with a minivan parked out front, indicating a family. Sure enough, inside the tent sat two open duffel bags, one belonging to a teenager about my size. I picked a rumpled church youth group shirt and shorts with an elastic band. I couldn't bring myself to don anyone else's underwear, so I went commando. I considered swiping a phone but decided I couldn't use it without linking myself to this minor crime. So, contrite at my necessary thievery, I said a quick "sorry" to the owners and exited the tent.

As I turned around, I came face-to-face with a raven perched on a nearby picnic table.

He tilted his head curiously at me. I froze. Maybe he was just a normal bird. They loved stealing chips and other treats from campers. He didn't necessarily have any ties to the kidama flock that had gathered outside Vincent's apartment.

At least, I could lie to myself until he squawked at me, spreading his wings as he took to the air in two quick strokes, sounding an alarm.

Somewhere, far in the distance, his buddies

answered, their voices combining into an angry choir. A gale whipped over the treetops, rustling the pines against each other in jagged spurts.

Uh oh. Very not good. I oriented myself toward the nearest wisp channel and made a break for it.

Fortunately, the raven had taken off in the opposite direction of the wisp channel. I had a head start on the flock. If I could wisp through to the other side, I could locate another wisp channel and teleport to yet somewhere else. Repeat the pattern a couple of times, and the birds wouldn't be able to keep up. I still had a chance.

I dashed under the canopy, the squawking squadron growing louder but only marginally so. I ran as fast as my bare feet could carry me, a decent pace actually with the earth cushion and my restored pithways. It felt good to be back at 100% again.

As I approached the summit of the last hill, I spared a glance over my shoulder to check my feathery chasers. An ugly black mass formed blob-shapes in the sky, swarming toward me. Scanning down the other side of the hill, I noticed the faint twinkling blue lights of the will o' the wisps. With gravity on my side, I could sprint away faster than they could reach me.

"Sayounara!" I yelled back at them, then stepped forward to execute my brilliant plan.

But as my next step met the ground, my foot smashed right through the dirt as if it struck wet paper.

I quickly sank up to the ankle in muck. I winced as I twisted at the wrong angle, momentum pushing me forward despite my leg being unable to bend that way. Instinct kicked in. I drew a quick earth sigil to yank my trapped foot free before I broke any bones, but I still stumbled down to my hands and knees. I tried to stand, but a pounding wind forced me to remain cowering on the ground.

My blood ran cold.

I forced my head upward, squinting in the wind to find Guntram between me and the wisp channel. He hovered a few inches above the ground through a continuous wind cycle, propelled by sheer fury. His shredded cloak whipped behind his bearded scowl, an expression I'd only ever seen him direct toward vaetturs.

So much for a clean escape.

I decided to give reason a go. "Guntram!" I yelled over the roar of the increasing wind. "Listen to me!"

He replied by raising his hands and drawing a series of sigils so fast, his hands blurred kung-fu movie style. The wind interference distorted the world between us, making the whole scene even more surreal. But the wind he generated was anything but intangible. It slammed my forehead so hard into the ground that I gasped.

The winds continued to howl, the pressure at my back increasing to a crushing weight. Clearly, explanations would not work here. I twisted my aching head to find Guntram gliding toward me on air, an angry god bent on banishing an unforgivable sinner. He kept my hands tightly pinned to the earth with two little wind funnels digging into my knuckles, a way to prevent me from drawing any sigils. With some painful effort, though, I managed to trace a simple square in the earth. I waited until Guntram perched only a few feet away before I finished the underlying slash. Then, instead of releasing earth pith out of my palm, I sent it up my spine straight out my forehead, creating an upturned line of earth toward my attacker.

Guntram never knew what hit him as the line crept underneath his hovering feet, undetected. Then it blasted up a radius of dirt. He sputtered and fell to the ground.

I leaped to my feet the instant the winds faltered. I wasn't an idiot. Guntram had decades of experience on me. I didn't stand any chance against him in a face-to-face fight. Even now, the winds bore down on me, just with a lot less force.

I decided to use that to my advantage.

I drew a quick sideways S and flung my air pith in the same direction as Guntram. Adding my own pith to his mix, I could steer it away from me, redirecting it in a sharp 90 degree turn at Guntram. He'd already recovered to his feet, but this unexpected blast with half his own pith truly knocked him sideways. He arched down the hill, away from the wisp channel lights.

I sped forward, running faster than I thought

possible. The distance, which once seemed so close, looked impossibly far away. As the lights bounced before me, I summoned a secondary wind at my back to speed me up a bit.

I did not expect near hundred mile per hour winds to smack me on the backside.

Guntram had pulled the same trick on me that I had on him, adding his air pith to mine. However, this brought me closer to the wisp channel, not away from it. He was helping me flee, I thought smugly. I'd be out of sight in no time.

And so, I sailed through the wisp channel, past the ground on the other side, and right over the shores of a large body of water. When the wind died abruptly, I crashed like an idiot down into the water's depths.

Because of course I did. Guntram had planned to dump me into the lake the entire time.

Not prepared for a dunk, I inhaled water as I tried to ascertain up from down. I allowed water pith to fill my lungs, my fingers flowing to draw the complex sigil to breath underwater. Water filled my pithways in a circular pattern, and I found myself weightless beneath the surface. Maybe I could dive deeper and hide. Surely Guntram would not find me in the relative darkness.

But before I could execute this scheme, something pulled me downward. Nothing touched me directly, but I sank way too fast toward the muck at the bottom. I tried to swim away but hit a swirling current that prevented my departure. That didn't make any sense. Lakes don't have currents.

But angry augurs can create them.

Guntram had created a vortex of water using whirlwinds, which flung water out of the mini-barrier he'd created around me. I soon found myself splattered with grime at the bottom of a very long cylinder that cut straight through the lake. Guntram flew above me, twenty feet in midair. We were encased in a tornado that spanned from the lake to straight up into the clouds. He drew a sigil to amplify his voice over the noise.

"It's over, Ina!" His shout rang in my ears.

But I couldn't accept defeat. Not now when I'd just gotten my pithways reopened, and by Tabitha no less. I had to go after Rafe and fix the mess I caused.

But the only way out was up and through Guntram.

I gathered my tired limbs and crouched in a tight, squatting ball, absorbing Guntram's wind directly back into me as air pith. I'd never mastered that long series of Ss that constituted flying like Guntram had, especially where he only drew an S every so often to keep suspended. But I had no choice. I launched all my stored air pith out of my bare feet.

I climbed five feet, then ten. Soon I found myself viewing the top of the entire lake. As I rocketed upward, I truly believed there was a slim chance I could make it. I had to keep drawing, find a way past Guntram.

But I didn't even get near him. He batted me back downward with a wind gust, a magical fly-swatter.

As I evaluated my minor injuries back down in the muck, Guntram's voice boomed again. "Either you come peacefully, or so help me, I will destroy your pithways once and for all."

I gasped. Guntram had planned to bind Rafe on Mt. Hood with a technique so dangerous, it could kill himself as well as his target. I may be willing to risk my own life to escape, but I balked at hurting Guntram.

I glanced back up at him, hoping to reason with him once again. But Guntram rose above me, an avenging angel riding the very heavens itself. I knew he'd do it. He'd never listen to me.

I surrendered.

CHAPTER 15

GUNTRAM CONSTRICTED MY hands by ripping strips off his tunic and wrapping them around my closed fists. He not only cut off the circulation in my hands, he made it impossible for me to draw any sigils. Then I swear he summoned every raven in the state of Oregon and had them swarm around me, leading me slowly to the homestead. He himself walked behind this little procession, hands up and ready to strike if I made the slightest wrong twitch.

Not that I could have done much surrounded by a living prison of birds, their irregular cries and flapping so loud that it gave me a headache. I considered making a run for it when we teleported through the first wisp channel. The ravens couldn't follow us, so I thought I might have a chance to sneak away, but even more birds waited for us on the other side. They would have pecked my brains out before I could do anything.

It took more than an hour to arrive at the homestead this way, and you can imagine the spectacle we made. Fortunately, only Sipho, keeper of the homestead, and her two mountain lions, Nur and Kam, saw us. They stood somberly in the forge doorway, outlined by its inner glow despite the day's brightness. My eyes met Sipho's briefly as we passed, but she turned sadly away like a funeral mourner after a coffin has been laid into the ground. A heavy weight settled in my chest as her intricate braids disappeared into the building.

I didn't know where Guntram intended to lead me. We bypassed the lodge, where shepherds normally rested. Instead, the ravens guided me to the large storage shed where Sipho kept all her farming supplies. I had no idea why as he nudged through the ravens and motioned me inside. The birds took that as a sign to roost, and they plopped themselves like little basketballs on the roof, making it sound like a bowling alley inside.

I sneezed in the relative gloom and stale air of the shed as Guntram pushed me toward the opposite wall. Despite the racket, I could finally have a conversation with Guntram.

"You gonna put me to work or something?" I asked skeptically, thinking of previous punishments I'd endured for breaking shepherd rules.

He snorted. "Hardly. Do you need to relieve yourself?"

That was a bizarre question. "No, why?"

He did not answer, unlocking the door of a closet I'd never given much attention to. As he ushered me into the six by six foot space, I almost faceplanted into a set of iron bars. Guntram leaned over me to open a gate, where he motioned me to sit on the only thing available—a straight-backed chair with arms made completely of metal. I did as directed, and he bent over to clamp chains on my ankles, bolting me to the chair.

"Hey!" I protested as I tried to stand but found I barely had enough slack to sit forward.

He shoved me into the metal backing and slapped two more chains on my wrists. Then he unhooked a pair of chainmail balls hanging from a nail nearby and slapped one each around my closed fists. The hooks of the mail had been designed as such that he could pull a silver string and tighten them to squeeze down over my closed fists. As he stepped back to survey his handiwork, I realized they were additional restraints on my hands to prevent me from drawing sigils.

Ultimately, I'd been encased in the perfect shepherd-holding prison. Strapped to metal and surrounded by wood floors, walls, and roof, I couldn't absorb much pith. What little air that circulated back into the closet didn't amount to much. And with my hands restricted, I couldn't cast any magic.

Guntram locked the bars behind him, silent as the Grim Reaper himself. I panicked as I imagined sitting here alone in the dark.

"You're just going to leave me back here?"

Guntram didn't quite meet my gaze. "It's only temporary until I hear back from Fechin and determine if the Oracle orders you bound."

My heart lifted at the 'if' in his statement. I opened my mouth to comment.

Guntram cut me off. "You won't avoid binding, Ina. It's simply that tradition dictates the Oracle give the command. Given everything you've done, it's inevitable."

He was thinking about Zibel catching me at the crevasse near Noti. "It's not what it looks like. I was investigating the recent earthquakes and—"

"I'm finished with excuses," he interrupted, his voice soft as a whisper.

The defeat in his posture was more terrifying than his anger. "Guntram, please hear me out. The fox dryant—"

Guntram sighed as he shut the door. I heard the lock click into place with a haunting finality.

My heart sank. So, there it was. As much as I wanted to believe otherwise, I'd failed Guntram in the same way Rafe had before him.

Why would he believe me?

* * *

Time loses meaning when you're in solitary confinement. I didn't perceive much except for the scratching bounces of ravens on the roof, a sensation I could have lived without. I tried to stay sane by forming any number of escape plans. I knew, even if Guntram and the others did not, that I had to stop Rafe.

I couldn't be bound here.

Still, it's hard to concentrate when you can

barely move, cooped up in the darkness. My thoughts veered from the mildly anxious to the downright crazy. Would the Oracle really bind me? If not, how many shepherds would disagree? Would a mob perform the ritual anyway?

At least I was so bone-tired that at some point I drifted off, despite being chained upright and mentally spinning out of control. Dozing calmed my mind until a glob of something cold and wet hit my cheek.

I snorted awake. A beam of light streaked from the doorway, revealing a mudball sliding down my shirt. "Hey," I protested weakly.

"Rise and shine," a sweet voice full of poison called out to me. "Traitor."

A small flame flickered in the darkness. It came at the end of a petite hand, which in turn connected to a fur-lined cloak that covered model-envious curves. She had a face to match, ringlets of platinum blond hair falling on either side.

Darby, Tabitha's former eyas.

I gulped. Darby wished for my death more than anyone. I tried to keep my tone as neutral as possible.

Instead, my voice cracked like a teenager's. "You need something?"

Darby sneered at me, her teeth gleaming in her fingerflame. "I wanted to see you for myself. The person who killed my augur."

I doubted telling Darby that I'd met Tabitha in some lava would change the young shepherd's opinion. Besides, I couldn't really blame Darby. I'd feel the same rage if her stupid shenanigans had resulted in Guntram's death.

Words wouldn't help, but I said them anyway. "I'm sorry, Darby. I didn't mean for anything like that to happen."

"Don't give me your apologies!" she screamed. "I deny them all!"

The earth trembled underneath the wooden floorboards. Darby had worked hard to train herself over the years. She could do some real damage to me, and I wouldn't be able to stop her.

I hoped to placate her, but as usual, the words came out harsher than I intended. "You're right. Apologies can't bring her back." I sounded too matter-of-fact, even to my own ears.

Darby's face flushed. "Then I can only avenge her, as she would wish."

The trembling increased to a dull roar underneath the metal chair. Everything around me vibrated to a fever pitch. Darby drew a flurry of squares, and by the murderous glint in her eyes, she meant to unleash something fatal on me.

And I could only sit there and watch her do it.

Just as Darby's fingers reached the end of her sigil, a flash of orange heat burst between us. Darby gasped and took a step backward into the shed.

"What is going on here?"

A cloaked female with a smoldering red bracelet and olive-green tunic emerged from the flame between Darby and me. I couldn't see her face since she had her back to me, but I recognized her no-nonsense voice as Azar, the fire shepherd.

"I…" Darby stuttered. The trembling lessened to a trickle. "I mean, I…"

"You should not be here," Azar reprimanded. "Guntram summons you. Go."

The shaking stopped completely. I heard shuffling, then a door slam.

Once Darby had gone, Azar whipped around to face me, dark hair barely visible underneath the hood. Her body shimmered from the fire flickering in her hand.

I nodded at her gratefully. "Thanks, Azar."

"Do not thank me. I've come to take you to the others. Fechin has returned."

CHAPTER 16

AZAR UNLOCKED ME from the chains and helped me stand. After sitting for so long, my joints protested, but Azar didn't give them time to adjust. She pushed me stumbling into the fresh midsummer evening. The sky welcomed me from the darkness. I took huge grateful breaths.

Azar led me to a nearby fire pit, currently a mound of simple ash. I felt a chill unrelated to the temperature as I took attendance of all the faces gathered around—Zibel, Baot, and Euchloe. Even Darby slid into place, hands folded, standing in the ring of her peers. Everyone who had fought against Rafe on Mt. Hood.

And none looked very thrilled to see me.

We all stood silently, Azar keeping close to me. The other shepherds cast fleeting glances at me, clearing their throats but not speaking. Darby would have killed me with her death glare alone. I tried to keep my chin up but found myself shuffling from foot to foot.

A voice cut through the awkwardness. "Thank you for gathering all at once."

Guntram came toward us, Sipho at his side. Fechin, his favorite raven, perched on his shoulder, cocking his head from side to side.

Azar's confident voice boomed in response. "Has the Oracle awakened?"

Guntram shook his head. "She remains in a comatose state."

My heart skipped a beat. The Oracle had been taken down on Mt. Hood. How could she still be out of commission after all these weeks?

Euchloe, a wind shepherd with a penchant for hyper spirituality, took a wispy step forward, her ethereal hair floating in the slight breeze. "Then why summon us, Guntram? Should we not stay at our posts?"

"Because we have a serious problem." Guntram gestured to me. "As you are undoubtedly aware, I have captured Ina, Rafe's possible accomplice."

"I am not!" I shouted back. I might have added more, but Azar wrung my arm. An uncomfortable heat made me wince, and I quieted before suffering burns.

Baot, a generally optimistic water shepherd with a hooked nose, brushed his long bangs aside with uncharacteristic nervousness. "'Possible accomplice?' Does that mean we don't know for sure?"

"She's conspiring with Rafe," Darby interjected. "She's admitted to it before." Azar tightened her grip so I wouldn't interrupt. I clenched my teeth to take the edge off.

Guntram nodded somberly. "Normally, I would wait for the Oracle to make the final call. Binding is a serious action, not to be taken lightly. However, given the extraordinary circumstances we find ourselves in and our shorthandedness, I feel compelled to discuss breaking protocol."

Zibel grimaced. "Does that mean no one else is coming from the north to help us?"

Guntram shook his head. "No. Since all activity is contained south of the Columbia for now, they want us to handle it. Everyone else is protecting the Oracle."

Sipho folded her arms. "You are the highest-ranking shepherd here, Guntram. Shouldn't this be your decision?"

"I would say yes, except I worry about the possibility of"—he glanced at me, finally—"bias. Ina was my eyas after all. I'd like to hear your opinions before making my final decision."

Darby didn't hesitate for a second. "We should bind her, immediately. Before she runs back to Rafe and hurts someone else."

Possible burn injuries or not, I couldn't sit there a minute longer and not defend myself. "I'm not working with Rafe. I'm trying to stop him."

I hissed as Azar lit up her fingers, but Baot stepped forward. "Wait. If we are to make a decision, I'd like to hear Ina speak." To my surprise, Sipho and Euchloe both nodded in agreement.

Azar hesitated until Guntram waved at her to comply. She let go of my arm. I sighed with relief.

Zibel glared at me. "If you're so innocent, how did you end up at the lesion I guarded?"

"I found the crevasse the same as you," I answered. "I followed the earthquakes. Why else would I show up after Rafe had already left?"

Azar regarded me with perfect posture. "Rafe has returned to previous lesions before. Indeed, that is why we guard them in the first place. We hope to catch him refueling his pithways."

"That's not what he told me," I replied.

A collective gasp rose from the crowd. It dawned on me how damning that sounded.

I focused my gaze on Guntram, since he was the one who really mattered. I had to remind him the kind of person I was. "You found me close to a new crevasse, right? That's because I'd tracked Rafe down there after he killed someone connected to that construction site on Mt. Hood. He's murdering people again using Nasci's lifeblood. I tried to stop him before he could hurt anyone else, but he got the jump on me."

Guntram held such a blank expression on his face, I could have used it as printer paper. "So you pursued him with pithways damaged after absorbing all that golem pith?"

"Not exactly." Here's where I knew I'd get into trouble, but I steeled myself to telling the truth. "After I left the homestead, I stayed at my parents. While there, the fox dryant visited me."

A groan escaped Zibel's mouth. Legs shifted and hands fidgeted. Why would they believe me? I'm the only one who had ever even seen the fox dry-ant.

Darby scowled. "Not this deceit again."

Something sharp pinched my pithways. I ignored it. "It's the truth. The fox dryant visited me, just like she did the first time I experienced ken. She struck me with lightning, and it reactivated my pithways. I could use a bit of magic again, however small. Knowing that you all don't think she exists, why else would I bring her up now?"

Darby stalked toward me so quickly that Azar moved slightly in between us. The blond shepherd stopped halfway, her hands up in a sigil stance regardless of my bodyguard. "Because you will say anything to worm your way back into our good graces, you little bitch!"

Wind snapped through the trees. Whether I or someone else caused it as tensions rose, I didn't care. I brought my own hands up, still restricted in chains, to face her. "Tabitha knows the truth. She asked me to stop Rafe, whether you believe it or not."

The ground trembled beneath our feet. I saw Zibel and Baot draw frantically to counteract Darby's shifting earth pith. Euchloe ran to restrain me on the other side of Azar.

I could have cared less about them. I wanted to rub Darby's face into it. "Rafe threw me into the magma. I met Tabitha there as a messenger of Nasci. She restored my pithways to their full power and told me to go after Rafe."

"That's impossible!" Darby cried.

"She chose me," I continued, not heeding the other shepherds' warnings to calm down. "Me, Darby. Not you, her precious little eyas, but the haggard she always hated."

That's when Darby exploded. Well, at least everything beneath her did. The ground sunk inches as dirt sprayed around us everywhere. She centered her sudden attack directly at my feet, leaving me at the epicenter of a crater meant to swallow me whole.

Except she couldn't. Anger could not overcome the most powerful shepherd among us.

"Halt!" Guntram yelled, executing a swift series of earth sigils.

The ground stopped shaking everywhere, except where Darby stood. There the earth opened up a bit, causing her to fall up to her waist before Guntram sealed her shut. Realizing the boundaries she had crossed, she stared wide-eyed up at Guntram.

"I-I'm sorry," she whispered to him.

"You're only sorry he's here to stop you," I said.

Guntram whirled around to face me. "Enough!" he boomed, the trees swaying like reeds behind him. Ravens cawed all around us, swirling as one united black mass in the sky. All the other shepherds jumped backward to give Guntram and me space to square off.

I stifled the urge to swallow. I tried reason again, this time with a more even voice. "Nasci chose me," I began.

But Guntram would have none of it. "I've made up my mind. He snapped his fingers at Azar and Baot. "Keep her subdued while I finish it."

The two shepherds conjured a ring of knee-high flames surrounding me. My heart raced as I realized what was happening. When I tried to step over it, they sprung to life higher than my head. Hands still enclosed, I couldn't summon fire pith to walk through it.

They'd cornered me for the binding.

I shook my head as Guntram approached the edge of the fire. "You can't do this!" I cried.

He raised his hands, already performing a series of complex sigils. "I'm sorry, Ina, but I can't trust any more of your lies."

He shot the first string of pith at me. It pierced right into my brain, causing a massive headache. Earth pith drained out of me, making me weak in the legs. I fell to my knees.

"You're making a mistake!" I screamed.

Guntram hit me without another word. This one resulted in a wave of nausea. I gagged, fire and air pith leaking out of me. I tried desperately to hold onto them, to keep them inside, but I couldn't resist the tug of Guntram's magic.

But I did feel something else. A familiar sizzle, filling the spaces that Guntram drained as he cleansed me for the standard binding ritual. Something behind me, beyond the flames, fed me lightning pith. Staring up at the sky, I noticed dark clouds in the distance rolling toward the homestead.

But no one else seemed to care, too focused on the unfolding drama inside the ring of fire. Guntram shot at me again. My water pith evaporated, but that just left more space for lightning to charge up every last nook and cranny of my now sizzling pithways.

Guntram's hands flew so quickly, I could barely see them. I did, however, notice the single tear stream down into his beard. He used his air pith magnification so only I could hear him whisper at my ear.

"It must be done."

Lightning sizzled at my numb fingertips. I couldn't move my fingers to draw a sigil, but then again, my hands were surrounded by metal chain mail.

Metal conducts electricity.

I straightened in defiance. "No!" I shouted. "Nasci choose me!"

I released the lightning directly out my fists.

Everything burst in a flash of pure light. A deafening boom rattled the entire homestead. The release of so much force knocked me, and I presume everyone else, over.

In the aftermath, a ringing overwhelmed my hearing. Wincing, I pushed myself upward. To my surprise, the metal balls and cloth crumbled off my hands in chunks. I'd obliterated them in the blast. It had only cost me the shredded top layer of my hands' skin.

Someone latched onto my shoulder. Guntram's beard loomed over me. I flinched, thinking he'd kill me on the spot. But instead of glowering down at me, he had his attention affixed on something else across the field. He'd turned ashen, eyes wide. I followed his gaze.

Underneath thunderstorm clouds, the fox dryant pulsated in alternating blue and white. The light accentuated the strands of her beautiful red coat and silver markings. Sparks flicked off from her snout. Both tails swished around her as she tilted her head to acknowledge not only Guntram but the other dumbfounded shepherds thrown in various states of shock.

Then, without a sound, she opened her mouth as if to cry out, baring her considerable teeth. A tree trunk sized bolt of lightning shot down from the clouds and struck her where she stood, causing all of us to look away.

And when the lightning faded, the fox dryant had vanished, taking the storm with her and leaving only scorched earth in her wake.

CHAPTER 17

IF THINGS WERE nuts before the fox dryant appeared, pure chaos erupted afterwards. Elements flew about in a whirl, the trained instincts of a group of seasoned shepherds. The ground trembled beneath my burnt palms, fire catching onto dry weeds only to be doused by cascades of water, and you could barely see anything through the sting of wind. People shouted to be heard over one another, their voices a mixture of panic and battle-ready commands. I curled up into a defensive ball, drawing defensive sigils around me to protect me from the magical confusion.

Finally, one shout rose above the din, amplified by an air sigil. "HALT!"

Guntram's booming cry quieted the natural elements. As a breeze blew away the remnants of smoke, I found myself in the middle of a loose circle of bedraggled shepherds, all in various states of sigil stances. From Azar to Zibel, they focused their wild gazes on me, all except for Guntram, who faced them instead. His hands worked in a blur to create a protective bubble over me. I belatedly realized that he'd shielded me from the majority of their attacks and probably saved me from death several times over.

Darby came to the same conclusion, her eyes the wildest of all. "Are you defending this traitor?" she demanded of my augur. "She tried to kill us!"

Guntram hands dropped to his side, dissolving the bubble. "The situation just became much more complicated."

Darby's jaw grew slack. "Did I imagine her blasting us with lightning?"

Sipho, flanked by both of her mountain lions, stood up. "You did not imagine it. Nor did you imagine the fox dryant, who supplied Ina with said lightning."

Indrawn breaths rippled through the shepherds. After years of dismissing my stories, they now had to believe their own eyes. I tried to sympathize with their position. Dryants generally do not hide themselves from shepherds, living amongst the very creatures they support. We visit them in the forests, the oceans, and the wilderness around us. Having one they'd never met before materialize out of nowhere, and wielding lightning to boot, was quite the shock. Pun intended.

But my sense of injustice overrode empathy. "I told you she was real."

Most of the accusatory glances shifted uncomfortably away from me, unsure given their blown presumptions. But not Darby. She stomped forward.

"Who cares? It doesn't change the fact that Ina's responsible for Tabitha's death."

Once again, Sipho came to my defense. "No, she is not. Ina may have been duped, but let us put blame where it is due. Rafe killed Tabitha."

This caused even more shuffling among the crowd. I gaped at Sipho. She took a big risk in defending me. I wanted to thank her, but she refused to look my way, focusing instead on Darby.

Darby glared at her. "I tire of everyone making exceptions for this filth! She's responsible for what happened on Mt. Hood. Nasci's will should now be done!"

Guntram bristled at her outburst, his cape billowing behind him. "Nasci's will is exactly why I cannot bind her."

Darby backed down under the bite of his response, but she still asked, "What do you mean?"

Baot, ever the diplomat, broke into the conversation with his upbeat voice. "Ina has been given her Shepherd Trial."

I gasped, only now realizing the truth. A Shepherd Trial is a personal test, sent straight from Nasci herself, to determine if you are ready to become a full-fledged disciple. Everyone present had received one as an eyas, so they knew the drill. Nasci plants a vision in your head, generally supported in some fashion by a dryant close to the shepherd. Given all the weird dreams I'd been having, Nasci clearly pegged me to stop Rafe. And with the fox dryant showing up not once but twice now (and this time with witnesses), no one could refute that I'd been set on the path to full-blown shepherd status.

The others recognized it too. Bemused and wary, sigil stances nevertheless relaxed, hands ran through hair, and murmurs rose.

Only Darby remained unconvinced. "It could be a trick. An illusion that Ina has perpetuated to blind you to her real intentions."

Sipho shook her head. "It is no trick. Though I cannot harness lightning, I can transfer its pith as well as any other element. That fox dryant exuded more lightning pith than even the wildest storm."

All of Darby's muscles clenched. She obviously wanted to say something, anything, but the words would not come. An awkward silence followed.

Azar broke it by clearing her throat. "What do we do now Guntram?"

Guntram's anger died down, leaving him pale, as if he had just recovered from the flu. "I am not sure."

Then he faced me, the first gleam of hope in his eyes since we fought near the dome. "Ina." He reached out to offer me a hand up. "There is much to discuss."

I didn't hesitate for a second. I latched on, letting him lift me up. He noted me wincing as torn flesh stung my palms. He ushered me toward the homestead's hot spring, leaving the confused group of my peers behind.

* * *

Nothing, I mean nothing, beats a soak in a natural hot spring. Warmed by geothermal sources, it creates the freshest batch of pith that can flow in and out of your body. Even after ten minutes of soaking, my palm's flesh had mostly sewn itself back together, the scar tissue fading with each cycle of elements whirling through my system.

I would have liked to bathe alone for an hour or more, but Guntram returned soon thereafter with a spare generic tunic. He perched on the pool's ledge next to me, hairy feet dangling in the water. He didn't care about my exposed cleavage, and honestly, I shouldn't have either. But I felt enough self-consciousness about my vulnerability—both clothes and situation-wise—that I slid up to my neck so the bubbling waters would conceal me further.

Guntram didn't mince words. "Tell me everything, Ina. From the moment you fled the homestead."

In a way, I did end up spending more time in the hot spring, just not in the relaxing fashion I wanted. I tried not to sound desperate as I reiterated all that had occurred: the strange dreams with Tabitha, the fox dryant's sudden reappearance, my team-up with Vincent to investigate the strange earthquakes. Guntram remained mostly silent, only asking the occasional clarifying question, so I couldn't tell how he interpreted my story.

He didn't seem particularly pleased when I described running into Zibel, nor my failed encounter with Rafe, but he didn't judge either way.

In fact, the only thing that truly got him worked up was my encounter with Tabitha in the magma. He shook his head as I described our conversation.

"That's not possible," he muttered.

"Look, I get it. The magma should have merged me back into Nasci like with Tabitha. But it didn't. And it didn't affect Rafe either. Actually, he's having no trouble tapping into lava like it's his own performance enhancement drug."

Guntram stroked his beard. "Perhaps it is tied with how you both absorbed vaettur pith. Your pithways may be permanently altered at this point. Maybe Nasci can no longer reclaim you when you are done."

I stiffened at this explanation. "Are you saying I've screwed myself over somehow?"

Guntram threw up his hands. "Who is to say? Nothing with you, Ina, ever makes any sort of sense."

I couldn't help but throw in a jab. "You mean, like the fox dryant? The one you've been telling me could not possibly exist?"

Guntram had the maturity to ignore my self-righteousness. Instead, his expression softened to one of melancholy. "I wish I could consult with the Oracle on this matter."

I thought of the Oracle, the most powerful shepherd with her unbelievable command of the elements, lying comatose. "How bad is she?"

"We believe she'll recover, but we don't know when. In the meantime, her absence has torn the Talol Wilds in two. The northern shepherds believe us southerners caused her condition, and therefore, should resolve the situation ourselves. They refuse to lend us aid until we either settle the situation or the Oracle awakens under their care."

"But that's ridiculous. The Talol shepherds are all on the same team. What's different now?"

"This time, it's not a threat from Letum but from humans. Even worse, a bound shepherd. And the worst yet of all"— he clenched his fists in his lap—"an eyas that I personally trained."

I hated how utterly defeated Guntram looked. Casting off propriety, I lifted myself partially up out of the water so I could throw my wet hands over his. "You can't blame yourself for Rafe's actions. He makes his own decisions."

Guntram withdrew his hands from mine. "Nevertheless, those are the facts."

"The fact is that he went off the rails despite your training, not because of it." I pulled myself completely out of the pool, drawing water sigils to dry my skin. I shook the folds out of the tunic Guntram had fetched for me and pulled it over my head. "Those northern shepherds really need to get their panties out of a twist.'"

A bemused smile crossed Guntram's face. "Do not lecture about emotions, Ina. Not with your track record."

"Okay, okay, point taken." I twisted my legs to sit cross-legged next to him at the edge of the pool. "But it doesn't matter what they think. It matters that we move forward."

"Agreed. Which is why I plan on sending everyone back to their posts at the lesions."

I raised my eyebrow at him. "I bet my dad's sushi recipe that Rafe won't appear at any place you're guarding. Not if he can create new magma sources whenever he wants."

"I realize now that we may not catch him as I hoped, but ultimately we are shepherds. The lesions are a direct attack on Nasci. We must tend to them as wounds, repairing Nasci where Rafe has rent her apart. It is our sworn duty to protect her above all else."

Ah, repairing the crevasses made a lot of sense, but it left one huge question. "Shouldn't stopping Rafe be our number one priority?"

Guntram leaned forward with his elbows on his knees, the water's surface lighting up his tired face. "It is. But nothing you said gives me any leads as to where he will go next."

I scrambled for an answer. "He said he would finish taking out Wonderland."

"By your own admission, he has already done so. The top two leaders of the company are dead by his hand, yes?"

"True," I answered slowly. "But he indicated he had more left to do."

"I find I do not have the mental capacity to predict a crazed lunatic such as Rafe. I will wait until one of my kidama catches him opening a lesion. If I can ambush him while he's vulnerable recharging his energy, I have a chance of destroying his pithways for good."

I sucked in a breath. "You're not going to use that awful binding technique on him, are you? It could kill you."

Guntram stood. "Better me than anyone else."

I didn't like this plan, not one bit. Not only did it rely far too much on luck, but Guntram's pained expression told me he planned on dying if that's what it took.

"Don't go all kamikaze on me," I pleaded. "At least let me dig around to figure out where he might go next."

Guntram sighed. "By all means, do what you think is right, but I cannot rely on you."

I leaped to my feet. "What do you mean by that? I've been given a Shepherd Trial."

He narrowed his eyes at me. "Indeed you have. I will not get in your way, but I will tell you now, Ina, that I do not have high hopes for you."

His matter-of-fact tone made my face flush. "You think I'm going to fail, despite everything I've been through?"

"Ina, let me be frank." The lines on his face tightened. "You create trouble wherever you go. I no longer know how to handle you. Even with your pithways restored, you haven't mastered all the elements. You're in the worst shape for a trial as I've ever seen an eyas. And the truth is, not all eyases pass their Shepherd Trial. Some even die trying. It is an absolute test of your worthiness, and at this point, I have no idea if you will succeed."

His opinion hit me harder than anything else he'd ever said to me. Guntram was not prone to exaggeration. He had already decided that I would fail.

"So, that's it? You're giving up on me?"

"Once the trial starts, there is no more mentorship," Guntram said. "No more tips, no more second chances."

I tried to keep my chin up, but my next words sounded breathless, even to my ears. "I can make it."

"I pray to Nasci that is true because from here on out, you are on your own."

CHAPTER 18

RECHARGING IN THE hot spring gave me a boost, but the combination of being held prisoner, almost getting bound, and Guntram's lack of faith took a toll on my mental state. I trudged to the lodge defeated, collapsing into one of the scratchy straw beds. I didn't mean to fall asleep, but I did, thankfully without the intrusion of goddess-fueled dreams.

I woke to a blue sky with twinges of darkness at the edges. I figured it must have been late evening. Given how refreshed my body felt, the nap did me a world of good. My pithways had the best flow I'd experienced in months. My stuffy head had cleared.

I was ready to face my Shepherd Trial.

I needed to contact Vincent soon. He hadn't spoken to me for the better part of a day, and with my phone dissolved in magma juice, I couldn't ring him up at the homestead. I'd have to find another phone.

But before that, I had to alert the other shepherds to Guntram's plan. Did they know he intended to destroy Rafe's pithways permanently by risking his own life? I couldn't imagine the others would approve of such a risky endeavor. Maybe if I explained it to the more sensible shepherds, like Baot or Azar, they could force Guntram to come up with a better strategy. Best case scenario, we might even formulate one as a team.

The lodge seemed empty, though, with no one in any of the rooms or the shared common area. Not unusual. Shepherds preferred the outdoors, some of the more hardcore ones sleeping directly underneath the stars even on the homestead. It wasn't late enough for people to retire anyways. Before leaving the lodge to search for them, I rummaged around the back of a hallway closet and found a stash of hoodie, shorts, and boots I'd tucked away a while ago. They didn't fit great on me, but I vastly preferred them to the scratchy natural fabric Sipho used in her homespun tunics.

Outside was more of the same, empty fields between sparse buildings with no sign of any shepherds. I frowned. I should have run into someone by now. I even stuck my face in all the homestead ponds, thinking fishy Baot might be lounging underwater. Nada. Not even ravens stirred in the branches or roofs of buildings.

With foreboding clenching my stomach, I made a break for the library. Even though I didn't want Guntram there studying binding sigils, I had to locate someone. But after unlocking the building with a combination of sigils, the interior remained completely dark. I lit a fingerflame and noticed a book left on a table near the door. It displayed the page with Guntram's awful permanent binding sigil, the deceptively simple hourglass strokes gleaming up at me through the flickering light.

Shivering, I walked back outside and finally realized something else was off. The sky had grown brighter since I began my search, not blending into sunset. And the sun shone in the mountains to the east, not the west.

It wasn't evening at all. It was dawn.

I couldn't believe it. I had slept away more than half a day. Glancing frantically around the homestead, I noticed the forge with its glowing windows and soft curl of smoke. I dashed across the field, knowing deep down I was probably too late.

I busted through the barn doors of the log cabin without any sort of warning. "Sipho!"

The forger didn't hear me at first, hunched over a work bench with her headphones on. She'd confiscated the Walkman from me years before, deciding she needed it more than me. I called her, waving my hands to get her attention, but she continued to fiddle with a small metal button underneath her magnifying glass. Below the table dark-furred Kam yawned and grumbled like a teenager, not happy with the hubbub.

Sipho finally noticed me as I rounded the table corner. She jerked her head upward in surprise, drawing in a quick breath. She recovered quickly, leaving the button on the table.

"Good morning, Ina. I am glad to see you well rested."

Well, that confirmed the time of day. "Where is everyone?"

Her eyebrows furrowed in confusion. "Gone back to guard their posts, of course. Guntram ordered everyone back last night."

My shoulders slumped. So much for my rallying plan. It would take days to track everyone down at their respective locations, if I could even find them at all.

Sipho frowned. "I assume you wished to speak to them?"

"Guntram's on a suicide mission. He plans to bind Rafe alone using a dangerous technique that could get him killed."

I expected Sipho to show some sign of shock, but instead she merely sighed. "That is unfortunate."

"'Unfortunate?' We have to stop him!"

"I'm afraid if Guntram wishes to journey solo there is not much we can do. He bears a heavy responsibility as the augur who trained Rafe. No one has been able to convince him that he is not at fault. Further complicating matters is his current authority as the highest-ranked member at the homestead."

I gaped at her. "You're not seriously going to let Guntram die because of the almighty shepherd pecking order, are you?"

She glared at me. "It is more complicated than

that and well you know it. You can only prevent Guntram from executing his ideals if you have a better plan. Do you?"

"No." I slumped down on a stool beside her, my arms draping over the surface in defeat. "I don't even know where to look for Rafe."

"Neither does Guntram. And we should be thankful for that, since he has just as much chance of facing Rafe alone as you currently do."

I let my head fall into the crook of my arms. "Wonderful," I mumbled through my skin. "Glad to know you have as much faith in me as everyone else."

Sipho tapped me on the shoulder. "What if I could aid you?"

I peered up at her. A mischievous smirk tugged at the corner of her mouth. I'd seen that expression before when she'd crafted a masterpiece.

The weight on my heart lifted a little. "You got something for me?"

She nodded, sliding the metal button across to me. "I do."

The bluish silver wafer had an iridescence that made the surface appear to shift under the lantern light. Its squat cylindrical shape with inward curve at the edges reminded me of something, although I couldn't immediately place it. Sipho had etched a series of bizarre sigils, lots of harsh jagged lines but clearly not the Vs of water. When I reached for the button, a familiar tingle lit up my arm.

I recognized the object. "You made a lightning

charm out of a lithium battery!"

Sipho smiled, pleased with my reaction. "And a rechargeable one at that. I had to infuse the original with metal I found in the mountains. The etchings are based on the sigil motions you use when you practice with lightning pith." She motioned toward it. "Please pick it up."

I hesitated, remembering how her previous prototype had blown up in my face. But I couldn't disappoint Sipho, not after she had stuck up for me when no one else would. I took a deep breath and clasped the charm in my hand.

The tingle in my arm immediately spread throughout my entire body. Instead of overwhelming my senses, as lightning pith normally does, it actually joined the other four elements in a pleasant buzz. I let go of it, and the reverberations slowly receded back into the charm, leaving my pithways without any negative consequences, not even a slight sting.

I whistled. "That's really nice, Sipho. For once, I feel like I can control lightning."

"That was the idea." She beamed. "A useful lightning charm."

I noticed the faint serial numbers etched in the metal. "Wait, how did you even get a lithium battery?"

"I used the currency you had hidden around the homestead, of course."

That's when I remembered that she had stolen my last emergency credit card not long ago. "You bought this with my money?"

Sipho scoffed. "I believe the trade-off well worth the price."

I held up my hands in apology. "No, no, you're right. This is fantastic." I rubbed the little button in between my two palms. An actual charm that not only held as much as my normal clunky batteries but also promised some control. "This is going to pack a powerful punch."

"I certainly hope so." Sipho flipped around to open a set of mini drawers behind her. "If you are truly on a Shepherd Trial to defeat a person who can tap into Nasci's very essence itself, you must utilize every advantage afforded to you." She handed me a silver chain with five dangling metal slats: one for each element and an extra for defense.

"A new charm necklace," I squealed with delight. I clasped it around my throat and sighed at its comforting weight. It was the magical equivalent of handing a ninja a satchel full of throwing stars.

Sipho threaded an extra chain off to one side and attached the lightning charm button through an almost imperceptible hole she'd drilled near the top. She patted my head as she surveyed her handiwork. "There. You are ready to take on any challenge."

Her confidence choked me up a little. I cleared my throat. "I wish Guntram felt the same."

Sipho squeezed my shoulder. "Poor Guntram

has the weight of Nasci herself bearing down upon him. I believe you were meant to unburden him."

Her attitude forced me to re-evaluate my self-pity. It was self-centered of me to think that after everything I'd done, Guntram would rally behind me. Sipho was right.

I had to prove myself.

I ran toward the door, eager to move forward. At the last minute I paused. "Thanks!" I called back to her.

"Do not thank me with words." She shooed me forward. "Get me a new cassette tape. I'm getting bored with my current music selection."

A goofy grin plastered on my face. "You got it," I promised. Then I raced out of the forge and into the Oregon wilderness.

CHAPTER 19

WITH THE SHEPHERDS scattered across the Talol Wilds, I'd have to figure out a way to track Rafe on my own, a daunting task. Before I could even begin my search, though, I had to contact Vincent. I'd been missing for a day. He must have had an aneurysm by now. Although I didn't have his telephone number memorized, I could look it up online.

I set a course for Carol and Dennis's rural convenience store. The owners knew me well enough from previous trips that they would probably let me use their phone. Located only a wisp channel away from the homestead, it would take less than fifteen minutes to get there.

Zipping through the thick underbrush, I flung myself through the twinkling lights to the other side. I emerged uphill from a rural highway. A good sprint would take me to the store. I strode forward.

Suddenly, I stopped. I could've sworn someone was watching me.

I hunched down into a squat, scanning the ponderosa pines. This part of the forest, though thinner than around the homestead, still boasted a decent density of trees. I strained my ears to listen for cars on the distant road, but not an engine stirred. The light breeze carried sounds of birds and squirrels going about their business, clearly not disturbed by any threat. That alone should have soothed my fears.

But it didn't. I pressed my fingers into the compost-like layer of debris that made up the forest floor. I sent my earth pith outward, scouring for vibrations in the woods around me. I sensed small animals, certainly nothing special. I had almost decided to bury my paranoia when a strong flutter reverberated toward me.

Something big shifted nearby.

Pooling fire pith in my free hand, I swung my head toward the vibrations. "I know you're there! Come out!"

A bush many yards away stirred. My fingers twitched. Rafe wouldn't catch me off guard again. I'd burn that mofo to the ground if he dared show his face this close to Sipho's.

It wasn't a human that emerged from the leaves, though, but a pair of thick branch-like horns. They rose higher, revealing a thin face with a wet, black nose. Wide ears and deep pupils completed the ensemble.

A black-tailed deer.

I let the fire pith flow back into the depths of my pithways. Sheepish at having been spooked by a creature of the forest, I let out a nervous laugh.

"Sorry about that. It's been a rough week."

The deer continued to stare at me with his un-blinking eyes. Animals generally don't judge like petty people do, but I squirmed under his gaze any-way. Tabitha's kidama had been black-tailed deer. She'd even imbued one of them as a dryant a few months back, but through a series of events (some of which I'd instigated), a vaettur had killed the poor guy. Add on Tabitha's recent death, and I wouldn't blame this deer for hating me as much as Darby did.

I didn't know what else to do, so I simply walked past the deer. He scrutinized my every step. I re-minded myself that this is just what deer do, but I couldn't help but shiver as I ran out of the tree line toward the highway shoulder.

My unease melted as I approached the aging structure that Carol and Dennis maintained. The signage came straight out of the 80s, and no one had bothered to pave the almost always empty parking lot. The familiar site erased all thoughts of the odd deer. I pushed the dirty glass door open to slide inside.

Carol glanced up from behind the front counter, holding a handkerchief over her nose. Her me-dium-length gray hair poked out underneath curl-ers. She wore her usual lumpy shirt with faded nametag.

"Hey, Ina." She sniffed. "Long time no see."

"Hi, Carol." I waited as she hacked for a spell. "You sick?"

"Yeah," she grumbled. "Summer cold. They're worse'n the winter ones. I hate taking these awful pills." She patted an open box of over-the-counter capsules next to the newspaper crossword. "They work, but they also make me feel fuzzy."

"Sorry to hear that," I said, my mind more focused on how to ask if I could borrow her phone. "Listen, can I ask you a favor?"

Carol leaned forward, raising a wizened eyebrow. "It's about that forest service fellow, isn't it?"

I flinched. "What?"

Carol fiddled under the counter. "He left you another phone."

My mind whirled as she plopped a small prepaid phone down in front of her. How had Vincent had enough time to leave me a phone over here, more than a hundred miles away from Florence?

"When did he drop it off?"

"Maybe two weeks ago. He was looking for you again. I told him I'd give it to you when I saw you. Got to worrying a bit about you too, myself. You usually drop by more often."

That's when it hit me. Vincent had probably searched for me right after the Mt. Hood disaster. He must have left this phone while I lounged about my parents' house. He'd been covering all his bases.

I let out a goofy giggle. "Yes! Thank you, Vincent."

Carol flashed me a conspiratorial smile as I powered up the phone. "He programed it with his number. Said to call him pronto."

"Perfect." I found his contact info right away and pressed the number. "Thanks so much, Carol."

"It's nothing to me, although Dennis thinks you two are a bunch of idiots. He wanted me to throw the phone away, says he's not running some dating service. I told him it's romantic."

My face reddened as the phone rang on the other end. I opened my mouth to clarify my innocent relationship with Vincent when the line clicked on to voicemail.

I sighed. Nothing was ever easy. I waited until the beep and said quickly, "It's me, Ina. I'm okay. Call me back."

"He'll call back, dearie," Carol reassured. Then she burst out into another horrid round of coughs. She excused herself for a drink of water and shuffled into the storage room.

I planted my elbows on the counter, head in my hands. What to do next? I had to find Rafe, but all I had was his cryptic little comment about Wonderland. Given that he'd destroyed the Mt. Hood resort site and created two executive corpses, I wasn't sure what other destruction he could possibly have in mind.

As I slumped farther down, one of my elbows slipped. I jerked upward, a discarded section of the newspaper slipping on the counter. The name "Foster" nearly jumped out of one headline. The full title read, "Wonderland Responds to CEO Foster's Death." Curious, I snatched the paper and unfolded the buried news item.

The article outlined Wonderland's recent string of internal disasters. Despite the death of company leadership, however, the acting CEO vowed the company would thrive. "Wonderland will survive, no matter the setback," Richard Caruso was quoted as saying. "Foster had a vision to create an outdoor-based adventure park on Mt. Hood, and his dream will live on." The article went on to list the millions of dollars in damages that Rafe's destruction had already cost. Stockholders were putting intense pressure on the company to resume construction soon.

Now I understood why Rafe had it in for Wonderland. He'd kept his eye on the news and probably anticipated the company would still build its resort on Mt. Hood. Rafe wouldn't stop until he'd tanked the company.

But where would he strike next?

I got my answer in the very last paragraph of the article. It said that Wonderland would proceed with a ribbon-cutting ceremony as planned for its new downtown office in Eugene. They offered limited tours of their supposed "eco-friendly" building to the public in the hopes of establishing community trust. The newspaper concluded that police would also be present, expecting protesters to show up as well.

I forgot to breathe. Rafe wouldn't attack a large crowd of people, would he?

But deep down, I knew he would. Rafe had declared at the crevasse that he would show people what "real shepherds" were capable of. I shuddered, thinking he would do that by making an example of a corporate office surrounded by a crowd of people.

I had to get to that ribbon cutting ceremony. I glanced at the loud ticking clock on the wood-paneled wall. It would start in under an hour.

A buzzing at my fingertips made me flinch. Vincent's number flashed on the phone's display. I fumbled in my haste to answer it.

"Vincent!" I cried. "I know where Rafe is going!"

But Vincent completely ignored my panic, too focused on his own. "Dammit, Ina," his voice choked. "Where have you been?"

My pulse quickened at the quiver in his voice. "I'm sorry. Everything's happening so fast."

Vincent continued without hearing me at all. "I drove all over Lane County looking for you. Hell, I must have searched Whittaker Creek over eight hours yesterday."

"Yes, I was there," I tried to get a word in edgewise.

"I haven't slept. I haven't eaten." His voice cracked.

"I'm sorry about that." I really was, even if my tone didn't reflect that. We had to get to Wonderland's headquarters pronto. "I called as soon as I could. Rafe's going to—"

His next shout shook me to the core. "I thought you were dead!"

I couldn't help but snap back. "That's because I was dead!"

Silence.

Trembling, I almost dropped the phone. Saying the truth out loud suddenly made everything that had happened in the last 24 hours more real. I got a grip on myself. I didn't have time for a pity party, no matter how much I wanted one.

My voice shook when I finally broke the silence. "I didn't mean to freak you out, but things prevented me from calling. Rafe sneak-attacked me at the earthquake site."

Vincent cut into my explanation. "You should have waited for me."

But I wouldn't let him bulldoze me like that. "Like the way you waited for me to check out Foster's accident? No, Vincent. You're a police officer. When things are dire, you have to act immediately. It's part of the job."

He grunted something indecipherable.

I pressed on. "But even though I should be dead, I'm alive. I swear I'll fill you in on everything, but right now, all you need to know is that Rafe is probably going to attack Wonderland's office in Eugene this morning. The company's doing some sort of PR stunt at their downtown office. I'm almost certain Rafe will be there."

"Are you sure about this? That's not his usual MO."

"He told me he's tired of working in the shadows. He's itching to make his presence as visible as possible."

Vincent went into full cop mode. "Then we've got to get down there. I can get there in a half hour if I hurry."

My heavy heart relaxed. "Thanks, Vincent. I'll meet you there."

But he had to get in one last dig. "You better be grateful, Ina. Because you are one stupid person to care about."

He hung up before I could reply.

I inhaled a shaky breath. "I care about you too, Vincent," I told the empty line.

Then I squirreled the phone away along with sentimentality. I mapped out the series of wisp channels that would get me to Eugene. My fingers grazed the lightning charm around my neck. It was my best chance of stopping Rafe. I wondered if I could alert Guntram and the others but couldn't think of how. All these concerns crammed into every corner of my brain, leaving no room for much else.

Which is exactly why I didn't notice Darby as I stepped out into the parking lot.

CHAPTER 20

TO BE FAIR, Darby didn't greet me with a smile either. She went straight to weakening the gravel under my feet, causing cracks in the dirt. The ground broke under my weight, threatening to trap me in place.

Years of training caused me to react instinctively. My legs flexed away from the softening ground, fingers drawing a string of Ss that blasted me upward. I leaped in a wide arc back to stable footing, away from the crater that formed where I once stood.

Darby stood near the trees. We locked eyes across the distance. Rocks fell from her hand as she reigned in her earth pith.

"Darby," I gasped. "What are you doing?"

"What Guntram can't." She slid her bare feet apart in a sigil stance. "What he refuses to do."

She flung two fireballs at my head. I skipped backward to dodge them, wondering why she meant to burn me when I could walk through fire. I got my answer when she followed the flame with two arcs of water, creating steam that acted like a thick mist between us. I could no longer see her, but the shaking ground indicated she hadn't gone far. I waited for it to crack beneath my feet, but it never did.

"We're not enemies!" I shouted. "I know where Rafe is going!"

"Of course, you do." Her voice drifted over me, slightly to my right. "You're in league with him."

The steam thinned out, and a vaguely human-shaped blob appeared where I'd heard her. "You think Nasci would send me the fox dryant if I was working with Rafe?"

Then the mist completely dissipated. It wasn't her standing there but a pile of loose rocks made to look like her.

"Nasci does not favor traitors!" she cried, suddenly right behind me.

I didn't have a chance to defend myself as a chunk of earth the size of a bowling ball struck the nape of my neck.

The defensive charm around my neck buzzed but did not shatter. It minimized most of the impact, which would have crushed my skull otherwise. Still, it left a big enough impression that my vision flashed as I whiplashed forward.

Darby didn't waste my vulnerability, flinging more massive stones at me. Even in my daze, I darted to the side, only a few grazing me. I couldn't let my guard down because I doubted the defensive charm could take another direct hit. I even managed to fling up rock walls between us to take the impact instead of me.

I scrambled to talk Darby out of her rampage. "Don't do this!"

"I won't let Tabitha's killer go free!" Her hands flew in a swirl of square patterns.

Sluggish, I attempted to sidestep the ground attack, but Darby anticipated my move. Before I could dodge to the side, she seamlessly transitioned into a hurricane gale slashing down from straight above, pinning me to the spot. Then she finished her earth sigil, plummeting me waist down into the parking lot's gravel.

I spread my arms out wide to anchor the rest of me from going under. I'd unburied myself before, but never with someone actively working against me, and definitely not someone with earth skills like Darby. If my hands became trapped in the dirt, she could easily wait out the rest of my air pith and suffocate me to death.

She stalked toward me, hands flying through another earth sigil.

"Darby, listen to me. Tabitha saved me in the lava. She doesn't want this."

"Don't say her name!" Darby screamed. The ground shifted again, encasing me up to the armpits now. I barely managed some counter sigils to stop her from fully entombing me in dirt.

I thought about giving one final plea but decided against it. I was sick of her drama. "Fine," I snapped. "You're angry. It won't solve anything. Trust me."

She flung her arms up, raising a boulder the size of a wheelbarrow out of the ground. "Spare me your pitiful life advice!" she shrieked as it wobbled in the air. "You won't talk your way out this time, Ina!"

I knew I wouldn't. She would bludgeon me to death with that rock, and I couldn't stop her. Darby was simply a more powerful shepherd than me. She'd earned it, training all those years under Tabitha's grueling pace. In her fury, I couldn't beat her with the standard four elements she'd already mastered.

I had to resort to the only one she hadn't.

Grabbing the lightning charm, I let its pith sizzle up and down my pithways. It jabbed at my insides with its coarse edges. My hair rose with static electricity.

"Then I'll zap my way out!"

Horror lit Darby's eyes, probably saving me from a boulder to the face as she paused in her sigil strokes. I focused my aim on that boulder, hoping to contain the lightning by pulverizing it but not directly hitting Darby. Thank God Sipho had given me this charm, otherwise I wouldn't have pulled it off. Even so, I prayed the charm wouldn't explode. I didn't want to kill Darby.

But I also refused to die.

The parking lot vanished in a roar of brilliant thunder.

Then silence.

I blinked away the afterimages of lightning

streaks, my vision slowly returning to normal. As darker colors crept from the outside of my vision inward, I saw crumbled dust falling like snowflakes all around me. As I coughed and breathed in tiny rock granules, Darby's slumped over form appeared, face down with her hair splayed out over her fur-lined tunic.

"Hey!" I cried, buried up to the armpits and unable to check on her. Scribbling squares within squares, I half-wriggled out, half let the earth push me upward. I crawled on all fours to get to her side. "Darby!"

My fingers pressed down into her hair, finding her throat. A steady pulse. I let out a long breath, then gently, holding her spine straight, flipped her onto her back. She looked like a mummy with a layer of boulder dust spattered all over her front, but I didn't notice any scorch marks. She had a nasty bruise on her forehead already turning purple. It must have knocked her out in the blast.

Hyperventilating in panic, I wasn't sure what to do next. I focused on a soft crunching sound coming toward me. Glancing back toward the forest, I saw a deer striding through the settling haze. I recognized the branch-like antlers of the black-tailed deer I'd run into near the wisp channel. His depthless black pupils locked with mine in a gaze that appeared to judge me. His hooves drummed out a steady beat, stopping only a few yards away from me.

But the unmistakable sound of hoof steps continued. More shadows formed behind the first deer. As my heart raced, I counted no less than two dozen deer emerging to form a semi-circle, all their gazes on me. I helplessly held Darby's head in my lap as these ghosts seemed to stand jury over what I had just done to a fellow shepherd.

Words refused to leave my heaving throat. "I-I..." I stammered.

The lead deer trotted forward, head bowed downward. I thought for sure he would stab me with his horns. I didn't even bother to avoid him. I merely waited for the inevitable.

He did touch me but not with his antlers. Rough, wet sandpaper tongue slashed across my forehead, licking my hair back.

"You're not mad at me?" I breathed.

He nuzzled my cheek in response.

I lost it then. Every ounce of emotion I'd held back poured out of me like water out of a sieve. Tabitha's sacrifice to save me, despite everything I had ever done to her. Guntram's crushing disappointment in my abilities as an eyas. Rafe's betrayal of my trust and all the damage he'd caused because of it. And now Darby trying to murder me. It all came flooding out of my weary body. I grabbed onto that poor deer's nape and wept, grateful that Tabitha's kidama forgave me.

And maybe I could forgive myself.

The deer let me hold him like a security blanket until my tears wound down to hiccups. I at least had the courtesy to wipe my nose on my hoodie sleeve rather than his fur. "Th-Thanks," I whispered in his ear.

He gave me one last nudge, then stood back up to his full height.

I gave a shuttering sigh, staring down at Darby. "She needs someone to watch over her. Can you do it?"

He pawed the ground in an affirmative response.

It took some maneuvering, but I managed to lift Darby's limp form up and drape her over the back of a random deer. Other deer gathered around us in support, a few of them even butting their heads around Darby's sides to help stabilize her position. Then, when I'd gotten her as secure as I possibly could, two more flanked the gurney deer, ensuring she would not roll off the side.

I rubbed the lead deer's nose. "You're sure you can handle this?"

In response, the deer jerked his head, and the two does at his side strode forward in perfect lock step as if members of a marching band. The others followed, including the trio carrying Darby. They trotted away at a decent pace, but I knew Darby would not fall.

As the herd slowly faded back into the trees, a loud creaking caused me to twirl around. Across the new shepherd-made potholes, the store's glass door inched open. Carol stood in the doorframe, gaping with mouth hanging down almost to her name tag. She watched as the last of the black tails disappeared into the woods.

"Is that...?" she asked, pale. "And you...? A storm...?"

I cringed. "Sorry for the mess."

Then I plunged back into the forest. Even if I could dream up a plausible explanation for Carol, I didn't have time. I had to catch up to Rafe.

CHAPTER 21

THE NEWSPAPER ARTICLE had mentioned that Wonderland built its headquarters along a section of downtown Eugene that bordered the Willamette River. It was all part of the city's long-term plan to transform a bunch of vacant lots into a "vibrant, active, and accessible riverfront district." Having attended a few semesters of college there, I translated that political speak for "get rid of the vagrant-filled abandoned warehouses along the tracks and replace them with nice businesses."

A wisp channel brought me near the northern banks of the river, a large wildlife area with lots of running trails and tree cover. I'd only ever used this portal once before, when Guntram had recruited me to become a shepherd in the first place. Scrambling up the river's embankment, I emerged not far from a famous track star's running trail. My mind flooded with nostalgia. I'd taken so many walks in and around this area instead of studying, trying to figure out why I could see strange animals that other people couldn't. It seemed fitting that Guntram had approached me along this very river to explain my burgeoning ken. I'd come full circle returning for my Shepherd Trial, yet still staring upwards at the same overcast Oregon sky.

I jogged down the trail until I crossed the pedestrian bridge. Instead of following the path toward the university, though, I headed west. My feet protested as my old boots pinched my heels. I wished the lava hadn't destroyed my last good pair.

I ran past a few empty lots and one large metal frame for a future apartment building before ending up at Wonderland's headquarters. Standing five stories tall with tons of curved glass supported by gleaming silver beams, the modern design appeared out of place next to the small motels and restaurants around it. Even if the building hadn't been screaming for attention like a prom queen at a cowboy ranch, Wonderland's six-foot-high logo with a skier swishing down a W would have been a dead giveaway that I'd found the right place. Two hundred people milled in the concrete courtyard, some holding cardboard signs. An empty podium had been set up closer to the entrance, roped off with a police car nearby to signal that everyone should behave.

I stuck close to the river, away from the crowd and unsure of how to proceed, when a deep voice called out to me.

"Ina!"

It took me a second to locate Vincent since he wore a windbreaker and jeans, easily blending in with everyone else. As he approached my remote vantage point, I flung myself at him before I could stop to think about it. So much had happened in a short time, and I needed the emotional support.

He immediately wrapped his arms around me in a fierce hug. "Glad I could finally make it before the fun started for a change."

A full holster underneath his jacket dug into my hip. "You brought your gun?"

"You better believe it." He pulled away from me. "I'm ready if that bastard shows up."

I raised an eyebrow. "But no uniform?"

"C'mon, you know Eugenians distrust the police. Look at them." He gestured toward the largely white, middle-aged people with their neutral-toned secondhand clothing. Several shot furtive glances at the police officers talking to each other at the bottom of the building steps. "I'd stand out as much as they do."

I swallowed, imagining Rafe trying something with this big of an audience. "Maybe I'm wrong. Maybe you're right and he won't show up."

"Yeah, well, I've changed my mind on that." Vincent pulled up the USGS database on his phone. "I got an alert about a 4.0 earthquake due east of Mohawk. It occurred less than a half hour ago."

"That's not good." Mohawk, Oregon lay northeast of Eugene, about twenty miles away. I'd probably missed feeling the earthquake's tremors during my fight with Darby.

Shouts erupted suddenly from the protesters. A business man in a suit emerged from Wonderland's large revolving door. Despite jeers and boos, he stepped up with confidence to the podium, a fake smile plastered on his chiseled face. The microphone squealed as he adjusted it to his mouth.

"Citizens of Eugene, my name is Richard Caruso, acting CEO of Wonderland. I welcome you to the grand opening of our new headquarters."

"Leave Mt. Hood alone!" a woman shouted when he paused for breath. This caused a wave of similar declarations, accentuated by a low-grade hiss.

Caruso continued as if he didn't notice. "We at Wonderland are pleased to welcome those who have completed an application in advance to tour our new building. Its certified LEED design reflects our commitment to sustainability as we usher in the future of outdoor recreation."

Cardboard signs shook at this declaration. "Stop old growth deforestation!" a rally cry went out as another group started a chant. Caruso seemed unfazed as he listed the platitudes of the architecture. The amplified speech and rising cries of the protesters soon collided in an inaudible soup.

I cringed. "Well this is just the worst."

Vincent scanned the crowd, but instead of a reply, his hand went for his holster.

"We've got company."

I followed his gaze toward the backside of the building. We were high enough that we could see behind the headquarters, past the river itself. An orange glow rose out of the muddy banks, growing higher and higher until you could clearly make out a humanoid figure outlined in fire. Its fathomless yellow eyes emerged as it burgeoned into giant form. Stumpy arms swung as it lumbered up the embankment toward Wonderland Headquarters, setting dry brush beneath it ablaze.

"What is that thing?" Vincent squeaked.

My heart raced. "A fire golem."

I tried to run forward to confront it, but Vincent grabbed my wrist. "Wait!" Dumbfounded, he glanced back at the ceremony. "Why isn't everyone panicking?"

I jerked out of his grip. "Because only shepherds can see it!"

"I'm not a shepherd! I can see it!"

The fire golem halted on the bike path. It straightened its chest and leaned its head back as if preparing to blow a little piggy's house down. Then its breath erupted with a roar, flames shooting straight at Wonderland Headquarters.

The fire collided with the building's third story. It set off a mini-explosion, glass raining down in millions of pieces, just barely missing Caruso.

Everything froze for a half second as numb brains processed the blast. Then panic ensued. Half the crowd ran away from the building toward the street while the other half stood dumbfounded in their tracks. Police officers grabbed those people nearest to the damaged building, pulling them farther away before returning to grab more. Unintelligible cries mingled with an alarm screeching inside the building, a slow trickle of office workers exiting as smoke billowed up into the air. Fortunately, given the slope of the courtyard, no one had wandered toward the river for shelter.

Vincent ran instinctively forward to help his fellow officers. He was trained to act in emergency situation. I, on the other hand, had no idea how to evacuate the masses. But as Rafe's minion took another step toward the building, I knew what I could handle.

I sprinted for the golem.

My boots pounded on concrete as I evaluated my options. I couldn't absorb the golem and risk ruining my pithways again. Been there, done that, bought the lousy T-shirt. I also didn't have the chops to disperse the golem, like Guntram could. I had to rely on my normal magical abilities to contain the situation.

As I spied the Willamette River gurgling below, I realized what might work.

I veered off the sidewalk, boots sinking into mud until I stopped only yards away from the golem's knees. It straightened its chest again, preparing for another wolf-like blow. My hands flew in a series of squares, but I needed more time.

I yelled, "Hey, ugly!"

It paused, neck crackling as it peered down at me.

Just enough time to finish the sigil. I slapped my palm down so fast into the mud that my fingers got temporarily sucked into the gunk. Full contact augmented my earth pith.

"TIMBER!" I screamed.

The entire slope of the riverbank suddenly slid downward, only me remaining stationary. Trees and bushes snapped in protest as they fell along with the sudden mudslide. The golem's clunky stump-legs couldn't keep balance with the abrupt shift. Flares shot out of its frame as it landed on its backside and gravity pulled it toward the river.

I had no idea how much water it took to douse a fire as big as that golem, so I didn't take any chances. Grabbing onto the water charm around my neck, I wrote a series of Vs with lines bursting out of the top, fusing my pith with the river down below. As the fire golem hit the riverbank, I released the sigil and conjured a leaping wave out of the river itself. It rose twenty feet and came down on top of the fire golem as it flailed for leverage to stand.

Steam and screams mixed together as water overwhelmed the fire golem. Grunting, I kept my legs spread in a sigil stance, absorbing as much ambient moisture in the air to renew my water pith. I had no idea if I could pull off a move like that again, but if the fire golem came back, I didn't have many other options.

As the steam cleared, I scanned for a flickering glow that would indicate the return of the fire golem. Instead of a giant, though, a human-sized shadow appeared. Rafe had decided to show himself. The scowl that marred his face made him appear almost like a caricature in his rage.

"You!" he yelled. "You should be dead!"

My jaw tightened. "Guess you're not the only special snowflake that can't die."

"We'll see about that!" One minute he looked ready to kill, the next he had drawn a rapid air sigil. He knocked me on my back so fast it left me breathless.

An ominous shadow bore down upon me. Rafe landed on me in a full tackle, then held me down by sitting on my stomach, hands pinning my shoulders to the ground.

Desperate to get him off me, I reached for the earth pith that should have been abundant around me as I lay in the mud. No matter how hard I tried, though, I couldn't absorb anything. In fact, all my remaining pith slowly seeped out where Rafe had his hands on me.

He was draining me of my very pith.

Rafe must have noticed my terror because a sick smile spread across his lips. "You can struggle all you want, Ina, but I have a lot more experience doing this than you. And when your pith's completely gone, I can murder you as easily as any other pitiful human."

I couldn't grab onto any of the pith in my system —not fire, air, water, or earth. Even my charms' pith faded away as Rafe immobilized me. Thrusting my head down, I could feel my chin brush against Sipho's lightning charm. Elated, I tried to absorb its energy into my pithways.

But I couldn't. In horror, I realized the lightning charm was empty. I must have used the entire supply during my fight with Darby.

I thought I was dead as the last of my pith drained away and into Rafe, but an ear-splitting crack interrupted the assault. Rafe yelped in pain and scrambled off of me. I crab-walked away to put some distance between us.

"Stand down!" a familiar voice called out.

Rafe clutched his left arm as Vincent towered over us at the top of the embankment. He held his handgun in both hands, its barrel focused on Rafe.

Rafe's wince slowly faded, replaced by a grin. He brushed himself off, casual as you please, not acting like someone about to get his brains blown out.

Vincent took a menacing step forward. "I will shoot you again!"

Rafe's hand slowly fell from where the bullet had struck, exposing his wounded arm. Where there should have been blood and exposed bone, only a trickle of magma oozed. It slowly glowed with an inner light until it faded away, leaving behind unmarked skin in its wake.

My throat went dry. Rafe had self-repaired somehow with Nasci's lifeblood.

Rafe raised both hands toward Vincent. "Your pathetic little firearm can't hurt me!" He drew a complex series of sigils.

I recognized him assembling another golem. "RUN!" I tried to warn Vincent.

But Vincent didn't have time as an air golem

189

emerged out of the sky. As it formed wispy arms and legs, it sent a wind gust at Vincent that put hurricanes to shame. Vincent flew horizontally, over the hill and out of sight.

"VINCENT!" I cried, trying to get up.

But a steady wind bore on top of me, keeping me down. Half of my face became buried in the muck while the other saw Rafe coming back for me, his newest golem rising as tall as his previous monster. Rafe's face betrayed his inner soul, a horrifying grimace of death. I grabbed at the elements around me, hoping to restore my pith for a fight, but Rafe jumped on top of me again. My minuscule pith stores drained away, leaving me completely vulnerable.

There was no speech, no grand gesture as Rafe closed his hands around my neck. He knew he'd have to kill me physically because I could absorb any elemental attack. I fought back against him, knee aiming for vulnerable spots like his groin. He avoided every strike. No punch would phase him. An awful glint lit his eyes, the kind generally reserved for kids riding a roller coaster. He experienced some sort of cheap thrill from watching me die, knowing I could do nothing as he squeezed the life out of my body.

My vision darkened as I weaved in and out of consciousness. Random images popped into my head. My mom hugging me under the lightning storm. Vincent's kiss. Tabitha berating me. Darby coming at me with a wall of earth. Guntram with

Fechin cawing on his shoulder.

The raven's caw grew louder.

The pressure eased.

Hacking up a lung, I pushed myself up out of the gunk. Someone stood next to me, not trying to kill me for a change. As I regained full control of my muddled brain, I realized this person wore a tunic and cape. He had his back to me but turned his head to reveal a thick black beard.

"Are you well, Ina?" Guntram shouted at me.

I didn't reply as the air golem threw all its magical energy at us, so forceful that I couldn't get my lips to surround my teeth.

"Guntram!" Rafe's wavering voice rode his golem's magic. The bastard had retreated to a safer vantage point to square off against his former augur.

Unlike me, Guntram seemed unaffected by the air golem's fury. He could have been standing inside the lodge on a breezeless day, his cape didn't so much as stir. He executed an air sigil that allowed his voice to boom out around us. "This ends now, Rafe! Surrender!"

Rafe answered with a rallying scream that had nothing to do with giving up. Guntram's hands flew in a blur as the golem's gusts intensified. I absorbed earth pith as fast as I could from the mud, drawing a sigil to allow me to stick to the ground before I flew away.

"So be it!" Guntram yelled, and he released so much air pith you could actually see strands of wind weaving together in a beautiful woven tapestry.

I couldn't contemplate its beauty as Guntram flung me away. I didn't understand why he'd tossed me aside until I watched him rip the air golem apart and, furiously scribbling, a gigantic tornado even taller than the golem shot up into the sky. It enveloped Guntram and Rafe, creating an elemental boxing ring where the two could face off alone.

I couldn't hear anything but whistling as so many invisible particles rushed past my ears. Nevertheless, Guntram's voice came in as gently as if we were having a leisurely soak in the hot spring.

"Go, Ina. I'll take care of this."

I couldn't mistake the melancholy in his voice. Guntram was preparing to sacrifice himself.

Then the tornado shut around both him and Rafe, leaving me on the outside.

CHAPTER 22

"GUNTRAM!"

Weak from asphyxiation and numb without pith, I shuffled forward toward that wall of wind. Guntram had wound the tornado so tight that although the gusts swiped me here and there, I didn't actually encounter true resistance until I tried sticking my hand through. If you've ever tried to swim against an undertow, you'd understand the sensation. Guntram had made a solid object out of motion. I had no idea how to get through it.

But I had to. Guntram faced a Nasci-fueled Rafe alone in there. Guntram would try to bind him using that awful technique. A deep anger surged within me. This was supposed to be my Shepherd Trial. My fight.

I would not let Guntram die for me.

I tried to push through the tornado by sheer force of will, each time more painful than the last. It nipped at my skin, threw dust in my mouth, and simply would not budge. I even opened all my pithways to let air flow through me, like I did in order to breathe underwater, but without an accompanying sigil to let me pass, all it did was make me dizzy and push me back toward the river's edge.

A huge magical surge threatened to overwhelm me, a cascade of all the elements together. The ground beneath me trembled as the river stopped flowing for a brief moment. That fierce pressure had originated from within the tornado. Rafe and Guntram were locked in some intense duel.

Why couldn't I get through? I stared upward at that column of air, frustrated with myself.

Realization dawned. I shouldn't go through. I should go up.

I'd never mastered the flying in air sigil, but I was an eyas to a wind augur. I couldn't fail this. Not now, when everything hinged on me.

Running my fingertips through the tornado, I absorbed a full fury of air inside my pithways. I didn't try to slow its velocity, letting it whirl inside me like a milkshake in a blender. As air dominated my pithways, my body levitated. My heels floated upward so only my toes touched the ground. Light-headed, I crouched down low in a tight ball, letting the dizziness overtake me. My fingers turned around in a long string of Ss, one after another until they blended into one another. I needed to become lighter than air. To shoot upward.

To fly.

Then, when my pithways felt as tight as an overstretched rubber band, I let go.

I realized belatedly that I still had my boots on.

The air blast ripped them to shreds as I shot upwards. Oh well. They'd been pinching me anyway.

I had other things to worry about. I closed my eyes to concentrate on the repeating air sigils. I didn't bother to measure my upward progress. I simply swept upward, fingers tracing unending Ss. I thought of Guntram, who until recently had believed that I could be a great shepherd. One who could make history if she could only control herself.

So, I controlled that air, letting out bits and pieces while simultaneously absorbing more pith as I paralleled the rise of the tornado. It wasn't unlike driving a manual car, shifting gears, slowly releasing the clutch, and stepping down on the gas. I became featherlight, accelerating upwards, not knowing if I'd made it ten feet or a hundred.

"CAW!"

My eyes shot open and I found myself face to face with Fechin. He flapped his wings furiously around me, the leader of a swarm of ravens that surrounded me. In the surprise of finding myself in a cluster of black birds, I faltered and slipped down a bit.

But the birds wouldn't let up. They flew directly underneath me, forcing me to steady myself or crush them if I lost my flight completely. Tugging on my pithways, I released a jolt of air pith that steadied me, narrowly missing one bird. Then I continued to absorb and release air at a rate that kept me stationary even as I floated high in the sky.

And I had flown up quite a ways, higher than the tornado that surrounded Rafe and Guntram. I'd reached all the way above the layer of clouds that covered Eugene. A vast sea of fluff spread below the pristine sky, the sun impossibly bright this high in the atmosphere.

"Whoa," I breathed.

I spotted the top of the tornado, its circular funnel creating a whirlpool of clouds not far below. Bits of firelight shone at the center of the vortex, indicating the epic fight occurring within.

I drifted over to the top of the narrow hole that led all the way back to the ground. I must have been a few thousand feet in the sky, and therefore couldn't actually see much as I peered at the empty space underneath my feet.

"Well," I said to Fechin. "Here I go."

Then I stopped expelling air pith.

The descent downward came so rapidly, I realized I would splatter on the ground without opposing thrust. I caught myself midway down, taking a second to finally observe Guntram and Rafe locked in their battle.

Guntram had encased Rafe in a mound of mud. In retaliation, Rafe had conjured a human-sized water golem that wrapped its body over Guntram like armor, covering even his face. Guntram floundered with cheeks full of air. Unable to move his fingers, he couldn't write an underwater breathing sigil, and thus, relied solely on his internal air pith stores for oxygen.

I resumed falling, more purposefully this time and at a reasonable rate. I waited until I hovered thirty feet above the pair before letting out a war cry and cut off all air pith. This gave me enough speed that I came crashing down almost on top of a bewildered Rafe. In fact, had Rafe not maneuvered the golem to intercept me, I would have crushed his fat melon head to pieces.

I apparently had not come solo. Guntram's ravens had followed me down the vortex, creating a virtual blanket of sable around us. I ran to check on a wet Guntram, releasing the last of the water golem's hold on my augur as the birds pecked Rafe on all sides. Rafe, unable to concentrate under the relentless assault, screamed as the birds pushed him directly into the wall of wind. The wind whisked Rafe away, straight off his feet and out of sight, vanquishing his golem as well.

With Guntram slumped over and dazed, the winds slowly died until they became sharp breezes whipping over the river bank. I kneeled next to him.

"Guntram?" I patted the cheeks under his closed eyelids. To my incredible relief, his chest rose and fell. He moaned, no water in his lungs.

With the tornado now gone, the sounds of police sirens echoed all around us. Smoke still rose into the sky from the fire, although the building remained out of view from where I sat. I had no idea what had happened to Rafe.

The birds settled around Guntram, Fechin land-ing at my side. "I need to go after Rafe," I told him. "Can you stay here? Keep him safe?"

Fechin's chest feathers burst out with several sharp caws. I interpreted that to mean he was insulted that I'd even asked.

Weak in the knees, I floundered up the slick, steep embankment to the edge of Wonderland's headquarters. No one appeared anywhere near the bike path, probably scared away by the sudden tornado. In the distance, the courtyard had been all but cleared save a few firefighters setting up trucks and ladders for the third floor. A glance at the street revealed a blockade to prevent new people from entering the area. I didn't see Vincent anywhere, which worried me, but I also didn't have a great view of the east side of the building.

Then I caught sight of Rafe, my prime target. He hobbled away from Wonderland into the adjacent half-constructed apartment building. He glanced over his shoulder at the police lights as he snuck behind a slightly open fence and disappeared out of sight.

"Oh no, you don't." I broke into an all-out sprint. I only tripped twice, absorbing as much pith as possible on the go. If Guntram had managed to injure Rafe, this might be my only chance to stop him before he killed anyone else. I thought I heard someone yell at me to stop, but I ignored them, not allowing local law enforcement to delay me at this critical juncture.

I wedged inside the perimeter of the construction site only to find Rafe gone again. The dark shell of concrete and metal didn't exactly make things easy for me, either. The crew had already put up the apartments' walls and roof, but the interior promised the dark gloom of a cave. With nowhere else to hide, I figured Rafe had slithered inside. I marched in after him.

Inside the framework felt like wandering around a half-finished labyrinth—lots of random twists but then some surprisingly open areas. Extension cords with electrical lanterns every few yards gave off a faint glow, but I still had to light a fingerflame to keep my bearings. I strained to hear any movement, keeping close to the walls and glancing behind me often. But nothing.

Rafe seemed to have vanished.

I rounded a corner and blinked as I came upon a brightly lit, almost warehouse-like space. The crew must have used this as a staging area, with various piles of beams, boards, and other materials stacked in the corner. A huge breaker box stood nearby with wires feeding off in every direction, an electrical heart with veins. The room had several doorframes to exit into other spaces, so I arbitrarily picked the closest one to investigate.

I chose poorly.

The moment I turned my back on the right door, a stream of fire smacked me in the back. It sizzled the base of my skull for a half-second before I tapped into my own pith and forced it to burn off in an arc. Wincing from a scorched neck, I switched to absorbing fire pith into my nearly-depleted pithways.

Once Rafe realized he hadn't caught me off guard, he switched to rumbling the ground beneath my feet. I crouched low and stabilized, letting everything else around me sway dangerously under his assault. The lights in the room dimmed considerably, but even so, I now had a clear view of Rafe leaning against a sawhorse. He rasped in exertion, striking eyes bloodshot and face gaunt, the result of his battle with Guntram. But he also had a fierce determination in his stance, the kind that cornered animals portray when they have nothing left to lose.

I waited for the trembling to stop before I announced, "It's over, Rafe."

"Is it?" he challenged. With surprising speed given his condition, he switched to a water stream that struck me in the hip. I gasped, half-absorbing, half-pushing it away.

Rafe knew how to leverage an opportunity. He resumed the earthquake, succeeding in tilting me backward. I kept my balance, though, redirecting the water stream at Rafe. He dodged it with a last-minute sidestep.

Rafe chuckled. "You can't hurt me. You don't have the pith!"

As if to prove his point, he shot a blast of air that nearly slammed me into the wall. As I strained to move forward, he suddenly let it go, and I stumbled right into his follow-up fire blast. That one got dangerously close to singeing an eyeball. A raw ache lit up my cheek. Stunned, I took too long to assess the damage. Yet another wind gust hit me so hard, it bashed me right into a corner of the breaker box. I cried out as it tore open a gash near my elbow.

I prepared myself for another elemental attack but misjudged again. Rafe closed the distance to grab my throat, choking me like he had before. He shoved me against the wall in such a way that he gained full leverage over me. I gasped like a fish, rasping for air even as he sucked it and all the other elements out of me. Using what little water and fire pith I'd absorbed, I tried to fling it back at Rafe, but they petered out from my stiff fingers.

That sick gleeful glint returned to Rafe's expression as I struggled. "This is your problem, Ina. You already know I can kill you, but you don't ever stop to think. You just barrel right ahead and attack, as if your will alone can beat me."

I slumped backward, hand smacking against the breaker box, which let out a hollow metal clang. As my fingers raked across the individual switches, a familiar sizzle shot through me.

Rafe increased the pressure at my throat, causing my lungs to scrunch in agony. "You have no magic, no one to save you. You will die right here like the bitch you are!"

I opened up my pithways. The electrical force felt too weak. Desperate to find a more powerful source, I slapped against the breaker box, searching for a strong current.

Rafe shifted, thrown into shadow so I could only see his awful smile. "Tell Tabitha 'hi' for me."

And that's when I located it.

A switch that surged as it crossed my pithways. I plunged my fingers through the plastic, making contact with the wires underneath. Electricity soared throughout my pithways. I drew a zigzag pattern furiously with my other hand, then pressed it up against Rafe's chest.

Rafe couldn't ignore the static flowing off me. "What are you—?"

I blasted him right in the chest, releasing a breaker's worth of electricity right through him.

Rafe screamed as he flew across the room and landed in a heap on the concrete. I scraped both hands across the breaker box, absorbing as much lightning pith as I could. It had the same potency as a natural lightning strike, maybe more even, but I found that I could control it better by carefully touching the many wires running through the box. As electricity accumulated in my pithways, long strands of my hair floated in front of me. My eyesight improved to a crisp, sharp focus, almost as if I'd put on special night-vision goggles. When I finally pulled myself away from the box, I grimaced under the strain of all that energy, sparks lighting off my elbows, fingers, chin, shoulder, everywhere.

I took a few heavy steps toward Rafe, lightning arcing between both my palms. "Still think I can't beat you?"

Rafe shrank like a frightened toddler. He knew he wouldn't escape this. "Please, Ina," he begged. "You can't kill me."

"Why not?" I growled, my voice distorted as if speaking through an autotune filter. I couldn't keep holding onto this lightning for long.

"Because you're not a killer. You love Nasci. I am her creation. You vowed to protect creatures like me."

"So did you!" My fingers itched to draw one final zigzag straight through his brain and get it over with.

"And Guntram did too!" Rafe wailed. Tears streaked down his face as he trembled in sheer panic. "Even he wouldn't kill me. Only bind me forever."

Every iota of my consciousness wanted to kill Rafe. I could fry him and there wouldn't be much of him left. And the rash part of me, the part that jumped into things on impulse, almost did it.

But I thought of poor Guntram. No matter what Rafe had become, Guntram refused to end his former eyas. He was even willing to try a technique that would kill himself first. I'd always admired his empathy before, his ability to see the good in things.

To see the good in me.

I would prove to Guntram that I could be a shepherd just like him. Instead of unleashing unbridled fury at Rafe, I etched out that awful hourglass sigil

I'd witnessed in the library.

If Guntram could risk his own life for this loser, so could I.

That didn't mean I couldn't make Rafe wet his pants for a split second. "Burn in hell, Rafe!"

Lightning webbed across the space between us, encasing us both in its crackling energy. But instead of cremating him on the spot like raw lightning would, a sick sensation shot throughout my pithways. The pith switched to a strange green light. Rafe's pithways lit up like an x-ray, revealing all the corners where he held Nasci's lifeblood.

Our energies locked together. I had no idea what to do from there. I could view Rafe's pithways, sure, but had no idea how to bind them. I hadn't paid that much attention to the tome that Guntram studied from.

In my hesitation, Rafe lashed out at me. Even crippled in pain, he managed to fling pith in the form of a fireball in my general direction. "You whore!"

Despite feeling like I might snap in two, I redirected my lightning pith to counteract the fireball. Lightning zapped not only the attack itself but the exact point where his pithways had stored fire. Rafe wailed like a banshee as a green firework exploded where my lightning struck. When the lights diminished, that corner of his pithways simply vanished.

Ah, so that's how it worked.

I became a human machine gun of lightning

pith, striking everywhere the green aura illumin-
ated Rafe's pithways. Sparks flew and thunder
crashed, drowning out Rafe's protests as I deci-
mated his magical system. It didn't come without
a physical toll on me, though. My muscles strained
as I continued my path of destruction. I even fell
down to the ground toward the end, running out
of lightning and unable to stand, but I soldiered
on. I refused to pass out despite blackness creeping
into the edges of my vision. I had to finish this,
once and for all.

When my final ounce of lightning pith struck
the last glowing ember of Rafe's pithways, I finally
let myself go. I crumbled to the floor, the concrete
cooling my sweaty face. I'd survived the hourglass
binding, but it had taken everything I had. All I
wanted to do was sleep for a year.

Rafe, however, wasn't done. Riddled with obvious pain, he crawled toward me on all fours. "Y-
you..."

"You're just a normal person," I finished for him
in a whisper. "No more magic."

"No!" he screamed. "I am a shepherd of Nasci. I
can wield the four natural elements." He clawed at
his bare arms. "I will find a way to restore myself. I
have done so before. And then, I will come for you,
Ina. I will destroy you and everything you hold
dear!"

He half-lunged for me, a wounded predator.

A loud clicking echoed over us. Vincent moved
in the doorway, handgun drawn and pointed

straight at Rafe.

"Stay down!" he yelled. "Or I swear my 'pathetic' little firearm will plaster your brains to the wall!"

I closed my eyes as Vincent read Rafe his rights and arrested him. I could rest.

Because this time, it really was over.

EPILOGUE

I WATCHED DARBY'S official shepherd ceremony from a hilltop far away.

They chose a spot close to the Columbia River Gorge to commemorate the event. All the shepherds that fought on Mt. Hood turned out for it. Even the Oracle came, having finally woken from her coma. She officially asked Darby to protect Nasci until her final days, and then unofficially brought white-tailed deer from all over the region to swarm the hidden waterfall. Everyone cheered and toasted the new shepherd with homestead mead. Euchloe brought out her harp and played a haunting induction song, but Baot's subsequent fiddle had everyone dancing as crowns of flowers were placed on Darby's blond ringlets.

Darby deserved it. Really, she did. Without her, I wouldn't be alive today. It didn't matter that she hated me now. I could silently cheer for her from above in the trees and pray that perhaps, with time, Darby would come around.

Because I was a full-blown shepherd too. I'd passed my Shepherd Trial by destroying Rafe's pithways. He would never hurt anyone again. And although a part of me wished for a celebration too, I wouldn't ask for one. I'd broken too many rules, caused too much trouble. Nasci's blessing or not, the others saw me even more as an outsider now than they had when I was an eyas. I was too much of a ticking bomb for them.

A rumble broke out in my kangaroo pouch. My phone. I had to go. I meant to duck away quietly back into the forest to the nearest wisp channel.

A familiar whisper in my ear stopped me in my tracks. "You do not wish to join us?"

I paused and glanced back down into the valley. Guntram had his arms folded under his shredded cloak, staring up in my direction. Very discreetly, he nodded his head toward the throng of dancing and laughing shepherds behind him.

I shook my head no, but it warmed my heart that Guntram had tried to include me. He was no longer my mentor, but he was still a high-ranking augur of the Talol Wilds. I would always admire him, and I cherished that he welcomed me as one of his peers.

But I had promised to be somewhere else, and I really needed to go.

I made it to the seedy little bar in Florence in minutes. There weren't any motorcycles outside, thankfully, and inside only a few tourists drank away their summer blues.

Despite arriving on time, Vincent was already there, seated in a booth with hamburger and fries already waiting for me. I slid into the bench opposite him with the largest, stupidest grin plastered across my face.

I pointed at the food. "It's like you know me, Vince."

He returned my smile. "I'm getting there. How did it go?"

I nibbled on a French fry. "She's a beautiful shepherd."

"That makes two of you."

I rolled my eyes. "You are so full of it."

He crossed his heart. "My word speaks only truth." Then he pulled out his cell phone to show me a recent news headline. "The grand jury moved Rafe's outstanding arson case forward. Not Foster's house fire but the beach one from months ago. Looks like there's enough evidence to convict him for that at least."

I scowled, thinking of all the grief Rafe had caused. Tabitha's death, Borden's drowning, Foster's car "accident," not to mention the many other crimes that had happened before I met him. "It's not enough."

"If he's convicted on arson, it's a start." Vincent bit into his own fish and chips. "Next up will be Foster's house fire. I'd love to be there when Rafe tries to explain the video security footage. Things will fall in place, and different jurisdictions will stick him with as much as they can."

I swirled the pop in my glass. "I should have done more."

Vincent took my hand from across the table. "I'm not sure how much more you can do in the criminal justice system. You're a nature wizard, remember? You beat down vaetturs and summon lightning. Most people would give their left foot to do that."

I sighed. "I wish things had turned out differently. That no one had to die."

His eyes softened. "I get it. I really do. I'm in law enforcement. We see the worst of people. Justice doesn't always get served. But every day, we have to get back up and go out there because if we don't do something about it, who will?"

He had the right attitude, even if my mopey butt didn't want to admit it. "I guess you're right."

Vincent leaned back in the booth, stretching a confident knee out into the aisle. "Of course, I'm right."

I decided to wipe that cocky grin right off his face. "That's not a nice thing to say on a date."

It worked. Vincent nearly fell out of the booth. "Is that what this is?"

"I don't know," I said honestly, leaning forward on my elbows. "Is it? Or should we keep this strictly platonic? I don't want to make things too complicated."

Vincent reddened but straightened, his dark eyes boring into mine. "Hell, it's complicated already. Why not?"

I nodded in complete agreement. Why not indeed. I really had no idea what the future held, not as a shepherd or with Vincent. I probably never would. But at the moment, I had greasy food, a real friend, and a charm necklace full of pith.

What more could a shepherd want?

WANT MORE INA?

If you loved Ina's story and want me to write more, please consider leaving an honest review on Amazon for this book. I have ideas for a follow-up trilogy for Ina's growing powers, and I will write it if I get enough interest.

You can also check out my next series, a portal fantasy that will take college dropout Avalon Benton from her minimum wage carnival job to a whole other world:

MAGIC PORTAL

You can also get a free *Magic of Nasci* short story by subscribing to my newsletter at dmfike.com.

ABOUT THE AUTHOR

DM Fike worked in the video game industry for over a decade, starting out as a project manager and eventually becoming a story writer for characters, plots, and missions. Born in Idaho's Magic Valley (you can't make this stuff up), DM Fike lived in Japan teaching English before calling Oregon home. She loves family, fantasy, and food (mostly in that order) and is on the constant look out for new co-op board games to play.

More places to keep in touch:

Website: dmfike.com

Email: dm@dmfike.com

Facebook: facebook.com/DMFikeAuthor

Amazon: amazon.com/author/dmfike

BookBub: bookbub.com/profile/dm-fike

GoodReads: goodreads.com/dmfike

MAGIC OF NASCI SERIES

Ina is a rookie nature wizard, learning the ropes of elemental magic—fire, air, earth, and water. She can also wield lightning, setting her apart from the other shepherds of Nasci. This action-packed urban fantasy series takes you on Ina's adventure to prove herself, deep within the heart of the Pacific Northwest forests, where true power still thrives.

BOOK 1: CHASING LIGHTNING

BOOK 2: BREATHING WATER

BOOK 3: RUNNING INTO FIRE

BOOK 4: SHATTERING EARTH

BOOK 5: SOARING IN AIR

APPENDIX: NAMES AND TERMS

This section contains a glossary of Nasci-specific terms and characters with pronunciations, presented in alphabetical order.

Afanc (aw-FAHNK): A beaver vaettur with crocodile features.

Augur (AW-ger): The second highest mastery in the shepherd hierarchy. Augurs have complete control over one element, have a special link to their kidama species, and can train eyas-level shepherds.

Azar (uh-ZAHR): A talented fire shepherd.

Banish (BAN-ish): To send a vaettur back to Letum using magical means.

Baot (bout): A water shepherd who spends most of

his time in the Pacific Ocean.

Bitai Wilds (bee-TAHY wahylds): The ecological region of desert encompassing the American West and Mexico that is overseen by a specific sect of shepherds.

Boobrie (BOOB-ree): A giant camouflaging bird vaettur.

Bound (bound): To seal a shepherd's pithways so that they can no longer access their magic.

Breach (breech): The interdimensional portal vaetturs create to travel from Letum to our world.

Charm (chahrm): An object that stores pith or recreates the properties of a sigil.

Cleft (kleft): An opening in the earth where vitae spills.

Cockatrice (KAH-kuh-tris): A dragon and rooster hybrid vaettur with a Medusa gaze.

Darby (DAHR-bee): A rookie shepherd with a talent for earth magic.

Dryant (DRAHY-ant): An animal with magical powers that guards others of its kind or territory. A dryant used to be a normal animal until it was blessed with Nasci's essence.

Etching (ECH-ing): A symbol that is marked on a specific object to give it pith or the properties of a sigil.

Eyas (AHY-uhs): A rookie (and the lowest level) shepherd.

Fechin (FE-chin): Guntram's favorite raven kidama.

Forger (FORJ-er): A follower of Nasci who can sense the four elements (earth, fire, air, and water) and redirect them into objects.

Golem (GOH-luhm): A creature made of pure pith.

Guntram (GOON-trahm): Ina's mentor and master air augur. Ina sometimes calls him Jichan (JEE-chahn), which means "Gramps" in Japanese.

Gyascutus (gee-uh-SKOO-tuhs): A wild boar vaettur with one side of its legs longer than the other to walk on hills.

Haggard (HAG-erd): A derogatory term for a shepherd that began training after puberty.

Homestead (HOHM-sted): A secret base with farms and other resources that shepherds visit to rejuvenate themselves and gather supplies.

Ina (EE-nah): A rookie shepherd with mysterious lightning powers. Her real name is Imogene Nakamori (IM-uh-jeen Nah-KAH-moh-ree).

Jortur (JOR-ter): One of Tabitha's favorite black-tailed deer kidama.

Kam (kam): Sipho's female, dark-coated mountain lion who's active at night.

Kappa (KAHP-pah): An aquatic humanoid frog vaettur.

Kembar stones (KEM-bahr stohns): Two stones that are linked like wisp channels.

Ken (ken): Magical sight granted by Nasci that allows a person to sense pith and see vaetturs and dryants.

Khalkotauroi (kal-koh-TOU-roi): A fiery bull vaettur.

Kidama (kee-DAH-mah): A species of animals that augurs can communicate with telepathically and give orders to.

Letum (LE-tuhm): The realm where the vaetturs originate.

Mishipeshu (mi-shee-PE-shoo): An aquatic feline vaettur with mysterious powers.

Nasci (NAHS-kee): The goddess that lives in the center of the Earth who grants elemental powers to her followers.

Nur (ner): Sipho's male, light-coated mountain lion who's active during the day.

Onyara Wilds (ohn-YAHR-ah wahylds): The ecological region of temperate deciduous forests of the Eastern United States that is overseen by a specific sect of shepherds.

Oracle (OR-uh-kuhl): The highest level of shepherd who leads all shepherds within a Wilds territory.

Pith (pith): The essence of fire, earth, air, or water that can be converted into magical energy.

Pithways (PITH-weys): A magical system that shepherds have inside their bodies to redirect and store pith.

Rafe (reyf): A mysterious stranger who shows up in the woods.

Ronan (ROH-nuhn): An antlered harbor seal dryant that lives on the Oregon coast.

Shepherd (SHEP-erd): A follower of Nasci who can store the four elements (earth, fire, air, and water) in their bodies and cast them using sigils. Also the third highest mastery of shepherd, just above an eyas.

Shepherd Trial (SHEP-erd TRAY-uhl): A rite of passage an eyas takes before becoming a full-fledged shepherd.

Sigil (SIJ-il): A symbol drawn in the air by shepherds to convert their pith into a specific magical spell.

Sipho (SI-foh): The forger of the southern Talol Wilds homestead.

Sova (SOH-vah): A northern spotted owl dryant with metallic mauve streaks in her wings.

Tabitha (TAB-i-thuh): Darby's mentor and master earth augur.

Talol Wilds (tah-LOL wahylds): The ecological region of temperate rainforests stretching from British Columbia to northern California that is overseen by a specific sect of shepherds.

Vaettur (VEY-ter): A predatory creature from Letum that enters our world to devour pith via animals and dryants.

Vincent Garcia (VIN-suhnt gahr-SEE-uh): A game warden for the Oregon State Police.

Vitae (VEE-tahy): The lifeblood of Nasci used to create new dryants.

Wisp channel (wisp CHAN-el): Glowing lights that shepherds use to teleport large distances.

Yoi (YOH-ee): The Oracle of the Talol Wilds.

Zibel (ZAHY-bel): A shepherd who spends most of his time in the Oregon Dunes.

ACKNOWLEDGE-MENTS

Writing a book is one thing, getting it out to the world is another. I'd like to thank those who read early versions of this story, including Jennifer Marshall and Sandra Schiller. You helped shape Ina into the awesome shepherd she has become.

Many talented people gave this book the professional care it deserved. I found my editor Lori Diederich through the 20Booksto50K Facebook group, an invaluable resource for new writers. Sara Smestad modeled for Danan Rolfe so we had plenty of great photos to choose for the cover.

A few final shout-outs. One to my first fan, Samantha Marshall, who believed before anyone else. The last goes to Jacob Fike, who lends both his time and skills to making each of my books better. I couldn't do this without him.